Alice in Blunderland

Alice in Blunderland

Phyllis Reynolds Naylor

SCHOLASTIC INC.

New York Toronto London Auckland Sydney
Mexico City New Delhi Hong Kong Buenos Aires

**To my granddaughter, Tressa Naylor,
with love**

No part of this publication may be reproduced in whole or in part, or stored in a retrieval system, or transmitted in any form or by any means, electronic, mechanical, photocopying, recording, or otherwise, without written permission of the publisher. For information regarding permission, write to Atheneum Books for Young Readers, Simon & Schuster Children's Publishing Division, 1230 Avenue of the Americas, New York, NY 10020.

ISBN 0-439-65033-X

12 11 10 9 8 7 6 5 4 3 2 1   4 5 6 7 8 9/0

Printed in the U.S.A.   40

First Scholastic printing, September 2004

Book design by Ann Sullivan

The text of this book is set in Berkeley Oldstyle.

Contents

1

Being Perfect

Lester lies to me sometimes, only he says it's just teasing. Then I go and believe him.

We were talking about names once, and he said he'd let me in on a secret if I didn't tell Dad. He said that we weren't Scotch-Irish at all, that our grandparents had escaped from Russia, but we didn't want anyone to know it.

My real name, he said, wasn't Alice Kathleen McKinley; it was Alicia Katerina de Balencia Blunderbuss Makinoli.

"Honest?" I said.

"Cross my heart," said Lester.

"Write it down," I told him. So Lester wrote it down for me.

I whispered my real name over and over so I could remember it. That night at the dinner table I watched my dad eat his green beans and wondered what other secrets he was keeping from me.

"What's Dad's real name then?" I asked Lester later.

"Hmm," said Lester. "That's a hard one to remember. It's Ivan Ilvonovich Rostropovich."

"I thought you said our last name was Makinoli."

"Right! Ivan Ilvonovich Rostropovich Makinoli."

"Then what's *your* real name?" I asked.

"Dmitri Rachmaninoff Schvaglio Deuteronomy Makinoli," said Lester.

I studied my brother. "Honest?" I asked.

"Would I lie to you?" said Lester.

"Honest *honest*?"

"Cross my heart," said Lester. "But it's a secret, and Dad's sort of touchy about it. He'll get around to telling you sometime."

The next day at school I couldn't help myself. Instead of writing Alice McKinley at the top of my fourth-grade spelling paper, I wrote Alicia Katerina de Balencia Blunderbuss Makinoli.

When we traded papers with the person beside us for checking, my friend Rosalind said, "What's this?" and pointed to the name at the top.

I thumped my chest. "Me," I said. "I just found out."

Rosalind looked at the name again. "Are you sure that last name isn't supposed to be Macaroni?"

"No," I said. "It's not."

Rosalind got up and went to the dictionary. When she came back, she said, "Do you know what a blunderbuss is?"

"No," I said.

"A person who goofs up," said Rosalind.

"Lester!" I yelled when I walked in the house that afternoon. My brother is about seven and a half years older than me, and he gets home from high school before grade school even lets out. "You just stuck 'Blunderbuss' in there. That's not part of my real name at all!"

"Imagine that!" said Lester.

"I'll bet you made that whole thing up," I said.

"How'd you guess?" said Lester.

I don't know why Lester couldn't have been a girl. Why couldn't I have had an older sister instead, one who would show me how to braid my hair and sew on a button and make fudge and cut my toenails?

My mother died when I was in kindergarten, and Lester and I live in Takoma Park, Maryland, with our dad, Ben McKinley. We moved here last year from Chicago. So instead of a big sister who could braid my hair, I've got a brother who plays the drums in a band called the Naked Nomads and tells me lies. I've got a cat, though, named Oatmeal, and that's our family— me and Dad and Lester and Oatmeal.

The fact is—and that's why Lester made me angry, I

guess—I really am a blunderbuss. Fourth grade is definitely the worst. I have already made more embarrassing mistakes in the fourth grade than in all the other grades put together.

Last Sunday, Dad took me to the mall and I had to go to the restroom. After I flushed, I tried to open the door of my stall, but I couldn't get it unlocked. I pushed and pulled, but the metal bar wouldn't slide. My father was waiting outside, but I would be stuck in there forever, I thought! They would have to feed me through the space under the door! I was too embarrassed to yell. Too embarrassed to pound on the door.

I could hear three women talking at the sink, and I decided I would wait until they had gone. Then I would crawl out under the door. I heard the women go out. I heard their voices fade away. Then I got down beside the toilet and crawled out underneath the door. There was still a woman left at the sink.

She gave a little gasp and turned around. I think she thought I was a dog.

"Hello," I said as I washed my hands.

She just stared.

On Monday, Sara, my second best friend, wanted to borrow a piece of paper at school. I handed her one. I had been eating a Hershey's candy bar the night before when I did my homework. There was chocolate on the paper.

"Euuuw!" said Sara, handing it back. "What's this? Poop?"

Everybody looked at me and laughed. I'll bet my face was as red as Sara's T-shirt.

On Tuesday we were eating beans and franks in the lunchroom. My mouth was full, and suddenly I sneezed. I sent beans and franks flying all over Megan's tray. "Euuuw!" said Megan, and she dumped her tray in the trash can.

Wednesday night it rained. I was in the bathtub when I heard raindrops pattering down on our roof. And right that minute I remembered that I had left my geography book on the front steps. It would be ruined!

I leaped out of the bathtub and pulled on my underpants. It was dark outside, so I ran to the front door, slipped out on the porch, and grabbed up the book. And there was Donald Sheavers from next door, taking trash to the garbage can. He saw. *He* says my name is Alice Kathleen Underpants McKinley.

Fourth grade stinks. Fourth grade is when everything you do embarrasses you. Fourth grade is when everyone knows you're a blunderbuss whether it's part of your name or not.

One morning at breakfast I said to my dad, "I'm going to try to go the rest of my life without doing any more embarrassing things. I won't do anything unless I think about it first."

"Good luck," said Lester.

"That doesn't sound like much of a life to me," said Dad.

"Why not?" I asked, my mouth full of scrambled egg.

"Because if you have to stop and think before you do anything, you'll never do anything spontaneous at all."

It seemed like more fun than being a blunderbuss.

Donald Sheavers came over to walk to school with me. He always stands with his nose pressed against the back screen until Dad invites him in. Then he sits and plays with Oatmeal till I finish my breakfast.

Oatmeal is a gray-and-white cat. The only things she does are eat and sleep and play and poop and pee. If you laugh at a cat because she does something funny, she'll just do it again. Cats don't get embarrassed, even when they throw up.

"I should have been born a cat," I told Donald Sheavers on the way to school.

"You might get worms," said Donald.

"Not if I lived inside," I said.

"You might get fleas," said Donald.

"Not if I never went out," I told him.

"You might get run over," said Donald.

"Not if I stayed in the house," I said.

"So who wants to live like that?" said Donald.

• • •

We have a man teacher in fourth grade. His name is
Mr. Dooley. Out on the playground some of the kids
call him "Mr. Dodo" or "Mr. Doo-bee" or "Mr. Doo-
doo," but he just smiles. We've only been in his classroom for two weeks, but Mr. Dooley never seems to
get angry. Donald says if you set fire to Mr. Dooley's
pants, he still wouldn't get mad.

He's not a blunderbuss, either. He never seems to
make mistakes. He doesn't spill food on his shirts or
forget our names or lose his attendance book or squeak
the chalk on the blackboard. I guess he's as perfect as
a teacher can be.

I decided I wanted to be like Mr. Dooley. Even if kids
made fun of me, I would just laugh.

Mr. Dooley thinks *we* are the weird ones. He says
fourth grade is a zoo. Except for Donald Sheavers and
me walking to school together every morning, the boys
and girls in fourth grade keep away from each other.

Mr. Dooley says boys and girls our age are like salt
and pepper. He says we are like north and south. He
says we are like magnetic poles that repel each other.
He says he likes teaching fourth grade.

But one day Mr. Dooley's car wouldn't start, and he
was late getting to school. The principal had to come
down to our room and take over until he got there.
And I could tell that Mr. Dooley had a headache when

he came in. His eyes were sort of squinting, and his eyebrows came together over the top of his nose.

"Donald, either sit on your chair the way it was intended or put it on your head," he snapped.

Donald put his chair on his head, and Mr. Dooley sent him to the back of the room.

There was a special guest in school that day who was going to talk about her books. We were going to be studying one of them in our class, and Mr. Dooley had been reading it aloud.

We were very lucky to have an author visit our school, Mr. Dooley said. When we joined the fifth graders in the all-purpose room, he wanted us to be on our best behavior. He wanted us to show them that we could be just as grown up as they were. I wondered if Mr. Dooley had ever taught fifth graders. Out on the playground they didn't seem very grown up to me.

We are never on our best behavior just before lunch because we're getting hungry. We were joking and laughing as we followed Mr. Dooley down the hall to where the author was waiting. As we giggled and pushed our way into the all-purpose room, the fifth graders looking at us, Mr. Dooley suddenly yelled, "If you don't settle down, I'm going to seat you boy-girl-boy-girl."

We were so quiet then that we could even hear Mr. Dooley's stomach growl as we passed him in the doorway. It was a loud gurgling rumble. We almost laughed, but didn't. We were so quiet, we could hear our own breathing.

The author smiled at us and thanked us for being quiet. She said she had written thirteen books and wanted to tell us about them. And then she did the most amazing thing. She accidentally burped, right into the microphone. Mr. Dooley may not have had any breakfast that morning because of his car, but I'll bet the author had eaten a very big breakfast because it was an awfully loud burp. Everybody laughed, even the fifth graders.

The author looked embarrassed. Mr. Dooley looked embarrassed for her. I felt horrible too. If teachers' stomachs growled in public and authors burped into microphones, this meant I would probably keep right on doing embarrassing things too for the rest of my life.

❀ ❀ 2 ❀ ❀

Phone Calls

A girl keeps calling my brother.

For a while we said it must be a ghost, because whenever Dad answered the phone, the person would hang up. When I answered, the person wouldn't say anything. She would just stay quiet on her end of the line until Lester got to the phone and took it away from me.

"Hello?" I kept saying, but she wouldn't answer.

"Lester, whoever that is, I wish she would either stop calling or start speaking. That girl—and I assume it's a girl—is driving me crazy," said Dad.

"Her name's Mickey," said Lester.

"His *girrrrl*friend!" I said.

"She's not my girlfriend," said Lester.

Once I thought it was Rosalind or Sara playing a trick on me. I could hear somebody breathing. So I said,

"Hey, stupid head. Are you going to talk or not?"

And finally the girl said, in a very soft voice, "Is Les there?"

"Just a minute," I said. I went down in the basement, where Lester was practicing his drums. The whole basement is Lester's bedroom.

"Les-ter!" I called. "It's Mickey Mouse."

Lester put down his drumsticks. He came upstairs and pulled the phone into the hall closet. When he came out, he said, "She's not Mickey Mouse, and she's not my girlfriend. She's just Mickey. Mickey Larson."

After that Mickey called a lot. She called when Lester got home from school. She called while we were having dinner. She called just before we went to bed.

For a while Dad didn't say anything more because he was glad Lester's making friends in Takoma Park. But one night we had just started to eat our pot roast when the phone rang again.

"Les, I wish Mickey wouldn't call while we're eating dinner," Dad said. "Can't you tell her not to call between six and seven?"

"Yeah," said Lester. That means he'll think about it.

The thing is, Les would never tell anybody not to call. Even if you don't like someone, a call from anybody at all is better than no call. The more calls Lester gets in an evening, the better he feels.

• • •

The Naked Nomads practice their music at our house sometimes. There are two guitar players, a cornet player, and Lester, playing the drums. Lester has a guitar, too, so sometimes it's three guitars playing, a cornet, and no drums. And sometimes the cornet player plays Lester's saxophone instead, so then it's three guitars playing and a saxophone.

They call themselves the Naked Nomads because they get so hot when they practice in our basement that they take off their shirts. And they'll go wherever someone wants them to play, so they call themselves nomads.

Rosalind's brother Billy is one of the Naked Nomads. She and Sara think they are silly. Sara thinks the band should get tattoos on their bellies or something.

"I think they should get tattoos on their butts," said Rosalind one day at lunch.

I laughed so hard I got milk up my nose.

When I got home from school that day, I went out in the kitchen where Lester was eating some leftover mashed potatoes.

"Sara thinks the Naked Nomads ought to get tattoos on their bellies, and *Rosalind* says they ought to get tattoos on their behinds," I told him.

Lester was reading the sports section of the newspaper, and he didn't even look up. "Tell your friends to go soak their heads in the toilet," he said. That's all he ever says about my friends.

. . .

The next time the Naked Nomads came over to practice, they worked on a song they had written themselves. The cornet player made up the melody, Lester
told us, and one of the guitar players—Rosalind's
brother—made up the words. Lester and the other guitar player worked out the arrangement; they decided
who would play which instrument.

The first time they played the music, it was so loud
that I could hear our windows rattle. A paper clip on
our coffee table started to jiggle.

Dad held his hands over his ears. I wondered if
Megan could hear the music two blocks down the
street. Oatmeal, our cat, was trying to sleep, but her
ears kept twitching back and forth.

"We will all go *deaf*!" Dad said.

He went down to the basement. He had to shout
four times before the music stopped.

When it started up again, it was just the guitar player
singing the words to the song and playing along on his
guitar. I sat at the top of the stairs and listened. Here
are the words:

"Hey . . . baby!
Hey . . . baby!
Hey . . . baby, wha'cha doin' tonight?

I . . . wan'cha,

I . . . wan'cha,

I . . . wan'cha, won't you hold me so tight?"

"Well," said Dad from behind his magazine, "at least it rhymes."

"How come Rosalind's brother is seventeen and he's a senior, and Lester's seventeen and he's only a junior?" I asked.

"Because we had Lester start kindergarten a year late. We didn't think he was ready, so he's always been older than most of the kids in his class," said Dad.

I thought about that a minute. This was something new! "You mean he was stupid?" I asked.

"No. Lester's always done well in school, but he was shy and immature for his age, and we felt we could give him a boost by starting him late."

"But he's got a zillion friends!"

"Just goes to show what holding out for a year can do for you," Dad said.

On Wednesday when I got home from school, Lester said he had to go to the library to pick up a book he'd reserved. We live only a half mile from the library. He said he would ride his mountain bike over and come right back.

I told him okay, even though Lester isn't supposed to

leave me home alone. That's the rule. On Tuesdays and Thursdays, I go to Donald Sheavers's house next door so that Lester can go places and do things. Donald's mom looks after me till Dad gets home. But on Mondays, Wednesdays, Fridays, and Saturdays, it's Lester's job to be there.

"You okay with this?" Lester asked, meaning I wasn't supposed to tell on him when Dad got home.

"I'm okay," I said, because I was having a good time playing with Oatmeal. "I won't start a fire or anything." I had tied a piece of folded paper to the end of a string and was dangling it higher and higher in the air to see how far Oatmeal would jump.

Lester hadn't been out of the house for five minutes when the phone rang, and I figured right away it was Mickey.

I cleared my throat and picked up the phone. "Hello?" I said, making my voice sound more grown up.

There was a pause, and then the girl said, "Is Les there?"

"I'm sorry, but Mr. McKinley is out. May I take a message?" I said.

"Who is this?" asked the girl.

"This is the secretary for the Naked Nomads," I told her.

"The *what*?" she said.

And I said, "Hey . . . baby! Hey . . . baby! Hey . . . baby, wha'cha doin' tonight?"

"You don't even know who I am," said the girl.

"Wanna bet?" I said. "And *you* don't even know that the Naked Nomads have tattoos on their butts." Then *I* hung up and laughed and laughed.

At school the next day I told Sara and Rosalind and Megan what I'd said to Mickey, and this time *Sara* laughed so hard that *she* had milk coming out of her nose.

I went to Donald Sheavers's after school, but later, when I got home, Lester was waiting for me. "Alice!" he growled. "What did you tell Lisa?"

"Who?" I said.

"Lisa! The girl who called yesterday while I was at the library." He looked over his shoulder to make sure Dad hadn't heard. About leaving me here by myself, I mean.

I swallowed. "That wasn't Mickey?"

"No, that wasn't Mickey! That was a girl in my history class, and we're supposed to work on a biography together."

I felt my lips beginning to separate as my jaw dropped.

"Why did you tell her you were my secretary?" Lester demanded.

"I . . . I . . ."

"And then she said you recited a poem or something. Al, what did you *say*? Tell me exactly what you said to Lisa."

My lips felt dry and I swallowed again. "Hey . . . baby! Hey . . . baby! Hey . . . baby, wha'cha doin' tonight?" I said, in a voice so soft, he could hardly hear me.

Lester stared at me. "Are you completely out of your mind?" he said. "She was calling to see if I got the book we needed for our biography. You made it sound like we're a family of idiots!"

He sat down on the couch, elbows on his knees. "Al," he said finally, "did you say *any*thing else to her? *Think! Anything?*"

I couldn't lie to my brother, no matter how many times Lester's fibbed to me.

"I told her that you . . . and the Naked Nomads . . . had tattoos on your butts," I whispered.

Lester buried his face in his hands. He wouldn't even speak to me till after dinner. I went down in the basement and told him I was sorry, but he said that not only was my real name Alicia Katerina de Balencia Blunderbuss Makinoli, but that I didn't even belong in our family. He said that somehow I got shipped to this country in a load of Russian potatoes, and no one knew what to do with me, so Dad took me in.

This time I *knew* Lester was kidding, but I'll bet he wished I *weren't* part of our family. I don't think he was kidding about that at all.

3

In Case of Fire

I don't like having to go to the Sheaverses' after school, but it's sort of a trade. Mrs. Sheavers looks after me till Dad gets home, and in return Donald gets free trumpet lessons at the Melody Inn. That's the music store where my dad works.

"Do you like to play the trumpet?" I asked Donald.

"I don't know," said Donald.

"Would you rather play something else?" I asked.

"Maybe," he said.

"What?" I asked.

"Baseball," said Donald.

The thing about Mrs. Sheavers is that she never lets us alone. She has to know what Donald and I are doing every single minute.

If she's working in the kitchen and we're quiet for

even a moment, she'll call, "*Don*-ald! *Al*-ice! What are you *do*-ing?"

Then Donald will tell her what we're doing—watching TV or working on a puzzle. Why can't people be left alone just to think, I wonder? Why do we always have to be *do*ing something?

Once Donald went in his room for a while, and I was in their living room by myself, reading a book.

"*Don*-ald! *Al*-ice!" Mrs. Sheavers called. "What are you *do*-ing?"

"*Breath*-ing!" I answered.

That night at dinner I said, "*No*body has to take care of me. I'm not a baby."

"I know," said Dad. "But I don't want you here alone in case there's an emergency."

"Like what?" I asked. "Like a fire? A tornado?"

"Like you might choke on a piece of hot dog or something," he said.

"If I was choking on a hot dog, what would Lester do?" I asked.

"I'd grab you by the heels and shake you up and down," said Lester.

That didn't sound right to me. I started making a list of all the emergencies I could think of, but only got to three when Rosalind called. I told her that Dad was worried about emergencies but I was worried about Lester. I didn't think he'd know what to do even if something bad *did* happen at our house. Also, I couldn't think of anything else except fire, floods, and tornadoes. Could she?

I shouldn't have asked Rosalind. Rosalind can think of things nobody else would even *want* to think about.

"You could always drown in the bathtub," she said.

I wrote that down on my list.

"The house could fill with gas and you could explode," she added. "You could catch your hair on fire or lock yourself in the basement."

Now I was *really* sorry I'd asked Rosalind.

"You could fall down the stairs and twist your neck or cut yourself on the can opener or lean too far out the window. . . ." Rosalind can think of things that have never happened before in human history. "Or," she went on, "you could get your foot stuck in the toilet or accidentally glue your eyelids shut."

"Rosalind," I said, "have any of these things ever happened to you?"

"No," said Rosalind.

"Then why do you think they'll happen to me?" I asked.

"Because you're a blunderbuss," she said. "Right?"

There was a fire drill at school the next day. I think I'm more afraid of the fire alarm than I am of a fire.

When the fire alarm goes off, you jump out of your

skin. Your heart pounds and your ears buzz and your brain melts and all you want to do is get away from that horrible noise.

"Get up and walk quickly out the door and to your right," said Mr. Dooley.

"Do not pass go and do not collect two hundred dollars," said Donald.

I held my hands over my ears to drown out the fire alarm. Outside we stood around waiting for the bell that means we could come back in again.

"Yay! The roof is on fire! No more school!" someone joked.

"Anybody got a match?" said someone else.

Mr. Dooley said that wasn't funny. He said if there really was a fire, we'd be smart to know what to do.

Two days later, just when I thought I didn't have to worry about a second fire drill for a while, there was another kind of alarm. This was a loud *beep* . . . *beep* . . . *beep,* a tornado drill.

"Go out the door, turn left, and stand in the hallway just outside the lunchroom," said Mr. Dooley.

We stood against the wall where there weren't any windows. You never know if a fire drill is real or not till you get outside, but we all knew that the tornado alarm was just a drill because the day was bright and sunny.

"Here we go, up in a whirlwind, all the way to Kansas!" somebody said with a giggle.

When we got back to our room, there was a fireman waiting for us. He said he was visiting all the classrooms to talk about safety and he would answer any questions we had.

I raised my hand. "What should you do if somebody falls out of a window or chokes on a hot dog?" I asked.

"Look for the nearest adult," the fireman said. That didn't sound much better than Lester grabbing me by the ankles and shaking me up and down.

I had to go to the Sheaverses' after school. Donald's mother had grape juice and vanilla wafers for our snack. Donald told her about the tornado drill at school, and I told her about all the emergencies Rosalind said could happen to me.

"Ha!" said Donald's mother. (When she says "Ha!" her earrings jangle underneath her reddish hair.) "I'd say Rosalind left out a few. What about all the *other* things kids think of doing? What about opening your mouth so wide it dislocates your jaw? What about crawling down a storm drain and getting swept out to sea?"

I stared at Mrs. Sheavers and then at Donald. Did mothers actually talk like that? If I had a mother, would she warn me not to open my mouth too wide?

Donald was reading a comic book. I don't think he even listens to her.

· · ·

I had just gone to bed that night when the wind grew stronger and stronger. Then it began to rain—a hard, October rain. Suddenly I climbed out of bed and padded down the hall to the living room, where Dad was reading a book.

"Hurricanes," I said.

Dad looked up. "What?"

"Hurricanes. That's another thing that could happen."

Dad patted the couch beside him with his big square hand, and I went over and snuggled up against him, against his soft gray sweater.

"Why are you so worried all of a sudden?" he asked, rubbing my shoulder.

"I wasn't until you said I could choke on a hot dog," I told him.

Dad grinned. "That's what you get for trying to talk me into letting you stay here alone," he said.

Then I told him what Mrs. Sheavers had said about dislocated jaws and storm drains. This time Dad laughed out loud.

"You know what?" he said. "I think that when there's only one parent in a family, that person has to do all the worrying for two."

I had forgotten, I guess, that Donald didn't have a dad. A live-in dad, I mean.

"What happened to Donald's father?" I asked.

"I'm not sure. They've been separated for quite some time," said Dad.

This, of course, made a worry of another kind. If I needed a mom and Donald needed a dad . . . I sat up straight and looked hard at my father. "Dad, *please* don't . . ."

". . . marry Mrs. Sheavers?" He smiled again. "I won't."

"But what if *she* wants to marry *you*?" I asked.

"Then I'll tell her I'm already taken," said Dad.

I stared. "Are you marrying someone else?"

He laughed. "Not that I know of. I'll tell her that being the father of Alice McKinley is a full-time job and that I can't add one more thing to my schedule," Dad said, and sent me back to bed.

I lay there listening to the wind and rain and thought some more about what he'd said. Did it mean that he didn't have time for any woman at all or just Mrs. Sheavers? That he wouldn't marry again till I was all grown up? That I might *never* get a mother?

4

Stomach Problems

I didn't go out trick-or-treating this year because it rained even harder on Halloween. Dad said I could go to the houses on our own block if I went with Donald. The first place we stopped at, though, gave us paper bags of popcorn, and by the time we got to the second house, they were a mess. The popcorn tasted like wet newspaper. I came back home.

Besides, I looked stupid. I hadn't thought of a good costume for our school party, so Dad had let me wear his old tuxedo jacket and gave me a baton, like an orchestra conductor.

"Who are you supposed to be?" everyone asked me. "A magician?"

"J. S. Bach," I said, because I'd heard Dad talk about him. I thought he was a famous conductor, but when

I got home from school, Lester said Bach was a composer who lived about three hundred years ago. So when I went out with Donald, I didn't wear any costume at all, and it looked like I was just begging.

If you miss out on Halloween, though, it's like missing a birthday. Like missing Christmas, almost. Now you have to wait a whole year for it to come again.

Lester wasn't sorry about it, though. Only two people came to our house for candy. "All these Snickers bars, just for me," he said, and took a handful to his room in the basement.

A week later, though, a nice thing happened. Megan Beachy had a sleepover birthday party. She invited her two best friends—Jody and Dawn—and me and my two best friends, Rosalind and Sara. At first she wasn't going to invite Sara because she says Sara smells. A lot of kids feel that way.

Sara *used* to smell, especially her hair, and it still smells sometimes if she goes too long without washing it. Most of the time, though, she smells like anyone else. It's hard for kids to change their minds about you, even after you change. But because Megan likes me and I like Sara, Sara was invited too.

Megan's little sister, Marlene, met me at the door when I got there.

"Put your present on the dining-room table and your sleeping bag down in the family room," she said importantly to each guest who arrived. She sounded like a teacher or something.

"No, not *there*! In *there*!" Marlene said when some-one walked into the kitchen by mistake. I decided I was glad I didn't have a little sister. A sister like Marlene, anyway. I was also glad that Sara had changed her shirt and combed her hair. I think she'd even squirted on some cologne, because she smelled like roses. Except that I don't like roses.

We all went down to the family room.

"Okay, everybody, you're going to play musical chairs!" Marlene said in a loud voice.

"Marlene, be quiet," said Megan. Then she shouted, "Mom, make her go back upstairs."

Megan's mother came to the doorway at the top of the stairs and looked down, and Marlene went over to sit on the bottom step, pouting.

We arranged five chairs in a row, and Mrs. Beachy put on a CD. Every time she stopped the music, we had to scramble for a seat. I was out on the very first try. Jody was out on the next, as another chair was taken away. Finally only Dawn was left. She got the prize: a necklace of orange and yellow glass beads.

After that we played a game called Scramble and ended up laughing in a heap on the floor. And after that we tried to see who could find the most number of words in *birthday* by mixing up the letters. Megan won that one, but her mother gave the prize to the girl who had won the next most number of words, and that was me. My prize was a baseball cap with WHAT-EVER printed on the front. I put it on so that the bill came down over my eyes, and everyone laughed.

We were tired of playing games after that, so we went upstairs and had pizza and carrot sticks with Megan's mom and dad and little sister. Then there was the birthday cake and presents.

My friends always like the presents I give them because Dad lets me choose cool stuff from the Gift Shoppe at the Melody Inn. He's the manager, so I guess he can do whatever he wants. For Megan I chose a tiny music box with a dancing bear on top. It went around and around when you turned the key.

At nine o'clock we put on our pajamas, and then Mr. Beachy played a video. It was *Harriet the Spy*, but some of us had seen it before, so mostly we didn't watch. We just lay on our sleeping bags and talked and giggled.

Marlene kept creeping downstairs, peeking at us.

"Go back upstairs, Marlene!" Megan yelled at her.

Marlene went back up, but after a while we heard the stairs creak again.

"Marlene, I mean it!" Megan called. She looked over at me. "I'll trade you one sister for one brother," she said.

"I have two brothers," said Rosalind. "One of them plays in a band with Alice's brother."

"The Naked Nomads," I said.

Everyone laughed.

"Do they get naked?" asked Jody.

"They only take their shirts off," I told her.

"I don't have any brothers or sisters. There are only three people in my family," said Jody.

"There are five people in mine," said Rosalind.

"Four in mine," said Megan.

When it was my turn, I said, "Just three."

"How can there be three if you have a brother?" asked Jody.

"My mom's dead," I said.

Everyone looked at me, everyone except Rosalind and Sara, who already knew. Megan knew too, I think. Everyone put on her "sympathy" face.

"How did she die?" asked Dawn.

"She got real sick," I said.

"Were you with her when she died?" asked Megan.

"No. She was at the hospital."

The kids were quiet for a moment, and their eyes looked sad.

"I wonder what it's like to be in a room when someone dies," said Sara. "Does an angel come to get you or what?"

"Oh, Sara!" said Rosalind.

"Well, anyway, you'll see her in heaven," said Dawn.

"I guess," I said.

Around midnight Rosalind got hungry, so we all went back upstairs for some more ice cream. Rosalind's as round as Sara is skinny. When we were done eating, Megan's mother said, "Settle down now, girls."

It was warm down in the family room, too warm to get inside our sleeping bags, so we just lay down on top of them. Rosalind said that if anyone's sleeping bag was touching anyone else's sleeping bag, the girls had to kiss, so we all screamed and pulled our sleeping bags away from each other so we wouldn't have to kiss anyone.

"Okay, everybody. Lights out!" Mr. Beachy called from the top of the stairs.

I was lying on my back, looking up at the ceiling where the streetlight made stripes through the blinds, and I was thinking about angels—if my mother was an angel. And suddenly my stomach made a loud gurgling noise, just like Mr. Dooley's stomach growled at school. It sounded like water going down the drain.

"Hey!" said Jody. "Whose stomach was that?"

Everyone laughed.

I didn't say anything. It happened again, even louder.

"Whose *is* it?" Rosalind giggled, getting up on her knees and looking around.

I breathed out. *Gurgle, gurgle*. I breathed in. *Gurgle, gurgle*.

Sara's squeaky laugh was loudest of all. "Let's see whose stomach it is!" she cried.

Now the girls were all crawling around over the sleeping bags, putting their ears to each other's stomach to see where the gurgling was coming from. I tried holding my breath to see if that would stop it. It didn't make any difference. *Gurgle, gurgle*.

I rolled over on my tummy. It went right on gurgling. My own stomach was a traitor!

"It's Alice!" said Jody. "She's got the growling stomach."

"Girls!" Mrs. Beachy came halfway down the stairs in her robe. "Quiet down now."

"We can't," Megan said, laughing. "We can't sleep because Alice's stomach is growling."

Mrs. Beachy shone her flashlight on me. "Do you need something more to eat, Alice?" she asked.

"No, I'm okay," I said.

"She needs some Pepto-Bismol," said Rosalind.

Everyone laughed again.

"Good night, now," said Mrs. Beachy. She went back upstairs.

Gurgle, gurgle, went my stomach. Somebody giggled.

"Al-ice! We can't sleep!" said Dawn.

I crawled into my sleeping bag and zipped it up, even

though I was too warm. You couldn't hear my stomach so easily from in there.

"Good night, everyone," said Megan.

"Sweet dreams," said Sara.

"Kiss a frog," said Rosalind.

"Don't let the bedbugs bite," said Megan.

Gurgle, gurgle, said my stomach from inside the sleeping bag.

While the other girls went to sleep, I lay there hot and sweaty and wondered how many embarrassing things had happened to me already in my life. Hundreds, I'll bet. Then I wondered how many were still waiting to happen.

Gurgle, gurgle, gurgle, went my stomach. I put my chin down inside my sleeping bag. "Shut up," I said.

My stomach wasn't listening.

5

Remarkably Awful

I didn't know how much I hated music class till I got to fourth grade.

Maybe I knew something was wrong back in Chicago. In second grade we had been practicing "The Merry Little Horses" for a PTA meeting, and the teacher stopped the music and had us sing it row by row. When she got to ours, she had us sing it two by two. When it got down to me and a girl named Margaret Keiler, the teacher asked me if, instead of singing, I might like to play the triangle. At the PTA that night, I held the triangle in one hand, the stick in the other, and at the end of each verse I went *ping*.

A week later Dad came to school for my second-grade parent-teacher conference. There hadn't been anyone to stay with me at home that day, so the teacher had asked me to copy some words on the blackboard at the back of the room while she talked with Dad.

At some point I'd heard her say, ". . . *remarkably* tone-deaf . . ." I remember feeling good inside, because anytime a teacher says *remarkably,* it must mean you're doing well.

But as we'd walked out to the car later, I could just tell by the quiet way Dad had his hand on my shoulder that *remarkably* and *deaf* didn't go very well together and that dad was feeling sorry for me.

"Am I sick?" I'd asked him.

"What?" said Dad.

"Is being tone-deaf like being sick?" I asked.

He'd laughed. "No," he had said. "You're a wonderfully healthy seven-year-old." And then he added, "I don't think you're exactly tone-deaf. You just can't carry a tune in a bucket, that's all."

But when I went to the doctor that fall for my checkup and he looked in my ears, I asked if my ears were okay.

"They look fine to me," he'd said, smiling. "Best ears I've seen all morning. Why? Do they hurt?"

"No," I told him. "But I'm remarkably tone-deaf."

He'd laughed. "My gosh, I can't sing either," he said. "The only place I'd sing is in the shower, so don't worry about it."

I figured if a doctor could laugh about you, you couldn't be very sick. But now that I was in fourth grade, I started worrying again. Maybe at Megan's birthday party I was worrying but didn't know it, though I realized the girls were looking at me sideways when we sang "Happy Birthday."

It wasn't until music class one day that I discovered for myself just how remarkably off-key I really am. We were going to put on a school assembly for Veterans Day, and each class was going to do something special. It was sort of a Columbus Day–Veterans Day–Thanksgiving Day program, actually. The sixth grade was going to put on a play about Columbus in the New World. The fifth grade was making a special pumpkin treat for everyone, and the fourth grade was going to sing "America the Beautiful," all four verses.

After we learned the words, the teacher concentrated on the notes. "Listen now, class," she said. She was a young teacher, and I'll bet this was her first year. We were sitting on the floor in the music room, and she was standing at the piano. She leaned over and played the notes to just the first few words: "O beautiful for spacious skies. . . ."

"Now, let's sing them really well," she said.

We all sang.

"I don't think some of you are *listening*," she said.

She played the notes again. "*Every*body. Sing the first note. A nice big 'O.'"

"Ohhhhh," we sang.

The teacher frowned. "Let's try it again. Just the people on this side," she said. She played the notes a third time.

"Ohhhh," they sang. My heart began to thump.

"Good!" said the teacher. "Now the people in the center." She made them try it. "Good," she said again. "Now the people over here." She played the first note on the piano.

The kids in our group sang, and I wanted to do my best. I sang out loud and clear. It sounded fine to me.

"Listen!" the teacher said, frowning even more. She played the note again. "Now try it," she said. We sang, but I didn't open my mouth quite so wide.

The teacher looked really unhappy. "Someone is singing much too low," she said. "Let me hear the four girls over here."

I was one of the girls. I sang, but not so loud. The other girls turned and looked at me. The teacher looked at me too. She played the note louder still. *I must be deaf,* I thought, and yet I could hear that note as well as anyone.

"Alice," the teacher said, "could you make your voice go a little higher?"

I didn't know what she meant by *higher.* I sang louder.

"No, not lower, dear. A little higher up the scale," said the teacher.

How do you make your voice go up? I wondered. I stretched my neck and raised my chin. When I sang the note again, some of the kids laughed. I could feel my cheeks begin to burn.

The teacher suddenly smiled at me and rapped her knuckles on the top of the piano. "Okay, class. *Every*one now, the whole first verse," she said, and it was then I realized I was hopeless. Nothing could be done for me.

When I walked home from school that day with Donald, he said, "How come your dad is manager of a music store and you can't sing?"

"How come you can't mind your own business?" I told him.

"I'm just *asking.*"

"I can so sing," I said in a tiny voice.

"Just not on the right notes," said Donald.

"Well, you don't always play the trumpet on the right notes either," I said. "I can hear you clear over at our house."

He just shrugged. "So what? I never wanted to play the trumpet."

"Then why are you taking lessons?" I asked.

"Because Mom makes me," he said.

I began to feel really awful. Donald had to take trumpet

lessons because his mom was taking care of me on Tuesdays and Thursdays. It was all so stupid. He didn't want to take lessons, I didn't want to go to his house, and I'll bet Mrs. Sheavers didn't even want me there.

"Well, I don't know why I can't get the notes right," I said finally. "They sound okay to me."

"When the notes go up, you go down," Donald said.

"Thanks for telling me," I said, and turned up the walk to my house. I was glad it was a Wednesday and I didn't have to go to the Sheaverses'.

Lester was on the couch with a bowl of pretzels on his lap. He had the peanut butter jar between his knees and was dipping each pretzel in the peanut butter before he put it in his mouth.

"I think I need an operation," I told him.

"What for? Somebody going to give you a new brain?"

I sank miserably down in my beanbag chair. "I think I need a new voice box or something."

Lester looked over at me. "Yeah?"

"I'm remarkably tone-deaf, Lester, remember? In music today it was horrible! The teacher made me sing a note all by myself, and Donald said I went down instead of up."

For once Lester said something really nice to me. "You know what?" he said. "Some of the people who can sing shouldn't, and if you *don't* sing, it doesn't matter."

I burst into tears. "It was so *embarrassing*!" I said. "She made me do it in front of everyone."

"Well, she shouldn't have. She should know that a lot of people can't carry a tune."

I wiped one arm across my eyes. "Will I get better, Lester?"

"I don't know," he said. "But it's not a disease or anything. Don't worry about it. Think of all the stuff you *can* do."

"Like what?" I sniffled as Oatmeal wandered into the room and climbed up in my lap. I stroked her as she pawed at my legs to find a soft spot.

"Well, for one thing, you take good care of your cat," Lester said.

"*Anyone* can do that!"

"And you make good popcorn."

"What else?" I said.

"Well . . ." Lester thought awhile. "You can blow your own nose."

"Lester!"

"You're a good reader. You have nice handwriting. You get good grades in spelling."

"But what am I going to do at the Veterans Day performance of 'America the Beautiful'?"

"Go to the teacher before the program and ask how much it's worth to her if you just lip-synch the words."

"What?"

"You know. Pretend. Just move your lips and pretend you're singing."

"Les-ter!"

"Well, just do it anyway. Just whisper the words. Who cares? It's America that's important here, right?"

"Right," I said.

The school sent home invitations to our parents in case they wanted to attend the program.

"Is this something special, Alice?" Dad asked. "Do you want me to come?"

"Not really," I said. "I don't know of any other parents who are coming. It's really just for the school."

"Well then, I think I'll stay at the store," said Dad. "We're having a big Veterans Day sale."

I felt better then. I didn't want Dad to come all the way to school just so he could watch me open and close my mouth like a goldfish, without one single sound coming out.

The program went off fine. I held my head high and opened my mouth wide, moving my lips as though I were really singing. And, since I was in the first row, I even put my hand over my heart and closed my eyes on the chorus, to show how patriotic I was.

Everyone clapped, and I figured if I could pretend I was singing the words, I could pretend that the applause was for me, and I even took a little bow.

6

A Houseful

Dad said we were going to have company for Thanksgiving. Janice Sherman, one of his salesclerks at the Melody Inn, didn't have any relatives in Maryland. And Loretta Jenkins, who worked at the Melody Inn's Gift Shoppe on Saturdays, didn't want to go out of town with her parents for the holiday; so she'd be alone too. So he invited them both to have Thanksgiving dinner with us.

"Loretta's the birdbrain with the sunburst hair?" asked Lester. He didn't want company for Thanksgiving. He wanted to *be* company.

"She's a very capable worker, Les," said Dad.

What Lester really wanted was to go to an all-you-can-eat Thanksgiving buffet at a restaurant so we wouldn't have to do any dishes afterward. But I was excited about having people at our house.

"I get to set the table for five!" I said.

"Make it seven," said Dad. "I invited the Sheavers, too."

"Dad!" yelled Lester.

"Actually, Mrs. Sheavers invited *us*," Dad explained. "And I thought it would just make things easier all around if I had them over here along with Janice and Loretta. Safety in numbers, you know."

"You could have asked me what *I* thought!" Lester complained.

"Mrs. Sheavers volunteered to bring the turkey," said Dad.

"Oh," said Lester.

It would be our second Thanksgiving away from Chicago. Last year we drove to Tennessee for Thanksgiving to see Uncle Charlie get married, and a few days later we drove back again for his funeral. He had a heart attack on his honeymoon, so I'm not sure how I feel about weddings.

"Everyone's going to bring something," I told Rosalind at school the next day. "There are going to be seven whole people at our house!"

"No halves?" said Rosalind. "No thirds?" We laughed. Rosalind always says crazy things.

"There are *thirteen* people coming to our house!" said Megan.

"I'm going to my grandmother's, and we're going to have twenty-two people there!" said Dawn.

I guess seven didn't seem like so many people after all.

On Thanksgiving morning Dad and I got up early and made the pies. We're good pie makers. We make pumpkin, pecan, and mincemeat. Dad buys the crusts already made, and we pour in the filling. Lester had brought home cider the day before. Here's what everyone was bringing:

Janice Sherman: mashed potatoes, cranberries, and green beans.

Loretta Jenkins: salad and rolls.

Mrs. Sheavers: the turkey, the gravy, and Donald.

Loretta looks sort of like a salad herself. Her hair, I mean. She was the last one to arrive, and her hair was all tossed and curly and wild around her face, like the fur on an Eskimo's parka. She's a little younger than Lester, and he pretends he doesn't like her, but Lester likes all kinds of girls except me. I noticed he sat right across from Loretta at the table and as far away from me as he could get.

"Isn't this fun!" said Mrs. Sheavers when we were all seated. She was wearing jangly earrings that reached all the way down to her shoulders. With her red hair and her green blouse, she looked more like Christmas than

Thanksgiving. "I know we're each thinking of things to be grateful for this Thanksgiving, and Ben's friendship is certainly high on my list." I looked at Dad, who was looking at his plate.

I'll bet Dad was grateful that he was at the opposite end of the table and Lester was grateful that Mrs. Sheavers wasn't our mom. Donald, though, was right across the table from me, and every time he swung his feet, he kicked me, so I wasn't very grateful about anything yet. Oatmeal kept walking from one chair to another, looking for someone's lap to jump up on, but we wouldn't let her.

"Now, tell me," Mrs. Sheavers said to Janice as she started passing the turkey around. "Just how did you come to know Ben?"

"I work with him at his store," Janice said, and it sounded as though little slivers of ice were coming out of her mouth when she talked. "I've known Ben ever since he moved here from Chicago."

"That's exactly how long Ben and I have been friends!" said Mrs. Sheavers. "We're neighbors, you know, and I take care of little Alice after school."

"Only on Tuesdays and Thursdays," I said. *Little Alice* made me feel like I'd shrunk.

If both Mrs. Sheavers and Janice Sherman were interested in Dad, though, he was too busy to notice, because he kept getting up to take things out of the oven or to put dishes back in to keep them warm.

"So, Lester," said Loretta from her side of the table, "what do you do with yourself when you're not in school?"

"Oh, try to stay out of trouble," said Lester, reaching for another roll.

"He plays in a band called the Naked Nomads," I said helpfully, because Dad told me to be part of the conversation.

Loretta smiled. "Naked Nomads? Hmm. Now *that* sounds interesting!" she said.

Lester gave me a look, but I noticed he smiled back at Loretta. It's hard to know whether I'm helping my brother or not.

"I can hear those boys practice clear over at my house!" said Mrs. Sheavers. "What a musical bunch we are! Donald here plays the trumpet, and I myself play the ukulele."

Janice Sherman lifted one eyebrow. "Really!" she said, only it wasn't the kind of *really* that sounded as though she wanted to know more. It was the kind of *really* that meant, *Not the ukulele!*

"What about you?" Lester said to Loretta. "What do *you* do when you're not at school or working at the Melody Inn?"

"I'm either at the beach or in the mountains," said Loretta. "I guess I'm a gypsy at heart. In summer I head for Ocean City, and in winter I go off to ski whenever I can."

"Sounds like a nice life," said Lester.

I noticed that Loretta was eating everything except the turkey. She didn't even take one slice. We found out later she was a vegetarian. I would have molded her a little turkey out of mashed potatoes if she'd just told us.

Dad had gone out to the kitchen for more rolls, but he'd left them in the oven too long, and they were burned on top. He went back for more butter.

Mrs. Sheavers laughed. "Poor Ben. He needs a wife, that's all there is to it."

She sounded as though she was joking, but Janice Sherman said, "Well, it would have to be an exceptional woman, because Ben's whole life, practically, is classical music."

Even a girl in fourth grade knows that what Janice Sherman meant by that was that Dad wouldn't be interested in a woman who plays the ukulele.

"Oh, but he's such a wonderful father!" Mrs. Sheavers shot back. "I'd think he'd be looking for a woman with maternal instincts. Alice is so in need of a mother."

How did I get into this? I wondered. "My dad isn't marrying anyone!" I said just as Dad came back into the dining room with a stick of butter. "He says that being my dad is a full-time job."

Dad paused there in the doorway, looking confused. "Have I missed something?" he asked.

"Only the rest of your life, which we're mapping out for you," Lester said, and everyone laughed then and pretended we were all friends. When Dad sat down again, though, he gave me a look that meant, *Whatever you were talking about, stop it!*

Okay, I decided. *I'll just shut up for the rest of the meal and see how they like* that!

But the pies with whipped cream put everyone in a good mood again, and when we'd finished eating and had cleared the table—which was nothing but a metal fold-up table—Dad got out the game Balderdash and the grown-ups began to play.

Donald and I went down the hall to my room. Donald picked up one of my books, *The Way Things Work,* and was looking up electromagnets while I sat on the floor with my back against the wall and worked on a bead bracelet I was making my cousin Carol for Christmas. I had started it two weeks before, but it still wasn't right. The trouble with homemade presents is that they always look homemade.

Donald sat on the edge of my bed to read. I think he's smart inside his head, but the things that come out of his mouth sound really stupid sometimes. Rosalind told him that Lester called me a blunderbuss, and every day Donald has to remind me of it, just because it's a weird word. "Blunderpuss" or "Blubber-bus" or "Bloody Pus," Donald calls me.

He looked it up and says that a blunderbuss is an old-fashioned gun with a flared muzzle. Great. I'm either a person who keeps goofing up or I look like a gun with a flared muzzle. Maybe something's the matter with my nose, I keep thinking. Nothing's wrong with the way Donald looks, though. In fact, he's probably the best-looking boy I've ever seen. If I ever *do* have a boyfriend, maybe it'll be Donald Sheavers.

Now Donald was reading to me what the book said about electromagnets, and then he began on rockets. I reached for another blue bead, threaded it onto the wire, and said, "Donald, what happened to your dad?"

Donald shrugged. "I don't know," he said.

"He just . . . left or what?" I asked.

"Yeah, but I don't remember him," said Donald. "I was real little, I guess."

I threaded another bead. "Do you miss him?"

"Nope."

"How come?"

"How can you miss what you can't remember?" he said.

I thought about that. If I didn't remember my mother at all, did that mean I wouldn't miss having a mother? I didn't think so.

"But wouldn't you *like* to have a father?" I asked.

"I guess."

Now I felt like teasing. "Would you like to have a girl-friend?"

"I don't know," said Donald.

"Do you want *me* to be your girlfriend?" I giggled.

"Okay," said Donald. Then he read me some more about rockets.

I was now Donald Sheavers's girlfriend, and I didn't feel one bit different.

Mrs. Sheavers came to the door of my room just then. "So *here* you are!" she said. "We *wondered* what you were up to."

"I'm making a bracelet and Donald's reading a book," I said.

"So I see," said Mrs. Sheavers.

"Alice is my girlfriend now," Donald told her, and turned another page.

"Oh?" said his mother. "When did you decide that?"

"Just now," I said.

"Well, why don't you two come out here and join us?" said Mrs. Sheavers. "You don't need to stay back here all by yourselves." Donald and I rolled our eyes at each other.

So Donald brought the book he was reading and I brought my bead kit to the living room, and we sat together on the couch with our feet on the big coffee table Dad got from Goodwill. The grown-ups went on playing Balderdash in the dining room.

"The only thing about being your girlfriend is, I don't want to kiss," I told Donald.

"Okay," said Donald.

It was easy being a girlfriend! I didn't have to do anything and neither did Donald. All we had to do was tell the kids at school so that Ollie Harris and the other boys wouldn't chase me at recess and Rosalind and Sara wouldn't chase Donald.

If Dad became Janice Sherman's boyfriend, I thought, maybe Mrs. Sheavers would leave him alone. I'd have to suggest that after all the company had gone home.

It was Lester I told that to later.

"Why doesn't Dad just make Janice Sherman his girlfriend, and then Mrs. Sheavers will leave him alone?" I said.

"Are you nuts?" said Lester.

"But it's easy! If you have a girlfriend, you don't have to do anything. You don't even have to kiss if you don't want to," I told him.

"What planet are you living on, Al?" said Lester.

When he says that, I know it's a dumb idea, so I never did give Dad my suggestion.

7

Excusing Mr. Dooley

Mr. Dooley was late to school again when we went back after Thanksgiving. Sara said he probably ate too much turkey and had a tummyache.

But when he came in around ten, he didn't look like he had a tummyache to me. He looked tired. Mr. Serio, our principal, taught our class until Mr. Dooley got there, and they stood in the doorway talking for a moment. Maybe Mr. Dooley was getting a scolding, we thought. But it didn't look like a scolding, either. Mr. Serio smiled and put one hand on Mr. Dooley's shoulder.

We did our spelling words and our arithmetic, but before we went to lunch, Mr. Dooley smiled at us and picked up a piece of chalk. He made a dot on the blackboard.

"Can anyone tell me what this is?" he asked.

"A dot," I said.

"A dot over the letter *i*," said Sara.

"Not exactly," said Mr. Dooley. He pointed to the dot. "This is the reason I was late to school this morning. Guess again."

We all stared at the blackboard.

"A flea?" said Donald. "Does your house have fleas?"

Mr. Dooley smiled. "No, not a flea."

"A germ?" said Rosalind. "Were you sick?"

"Not a germ," said Mr. Dooley. He pointed to the thing he had drawn. "This is the way a baby begins, just a ball of cells no bigger than a dot inside its mother. My wife is going to have a baby, and she doesn't sleep very well at night, so neither do I." He smiled again. "And that's why I was late. I overslept this morning."

He looked pretty happy for a man who was missing his sleep. "This is our first child," Mr. Dooley said, "so we're very excited."

We were excited too, and we were ready to excuse Mr. Dooley anytime he was late from now on.

"When will it be born?" asked Ollie.

"In April," said Mr. Dooley. "April twelfth, the doctor says. It takes nine months for a baby to be ready to be born, class." He turned to the blackboard again and wrote *July* over the dot. Next he drew something the size of a pea, and over the pea he wrote *August*.

"When it's a month old, it's this big," he said, pointing to the pea. "It's backbone has begun to grow and its heart has started to beat."

Mr. Dooley drew a lima bean next and wrote *September* over it. He pointed to the lima bean. "When it's inside its mother for two months, it's started to get its fingers and toes and ears and eyes and nose and lips. Even its eyelids."

He drew a peach and wrote *October.* "Here it's getting its fingernails and toenails, and here"—he drew something the size of a grapefruit—"is the size of our baby right now."

He smiled some more. "In our science unit we'll be studying how things grow—seeds and eggs and birds and babies. And each month I'll tell you how our baby is doing. Does anyone know what we call a baby when it is very, very small inside its mother?"

"A seed?" said Dawn.

"No, not a seed."

I knew the answer to that and held up my hand. "An embargo," I said.

Mr. Dooley laughed. Several kids turned around and grinned.

"Not quite," said Mr. Dooley. "An embryo. For the first nine weeks inside its mother, it is in the embryonic stage, and after that, until it's ready to be born, we call it a fetus."

Why did I say *embargo?* I wondered, my cheeks red. But Mr. Dooley went right on talking.

"Does anyone know which animal spends the longest time inside its mother before it's born?"

"A dinosaur?" asked Donald.

"Well, we're not too sure about dinosaurs, but you may be right," said Mr. Dooley.

"An elephant," said Rosalind, who wants to work in a zoo.

"Right! Very good!" Mr. Dooley said. "An elephant baby stays about six hundred and sixty days inside its mother."

"Wow!" we said.

"What's the shortest time a baby stays inside its mother?" asked Ollie.

"Good question!" said Mr. Dooley. "But I'm not going to tell you. That will be your science homework tonight. Find out what animal stays inside its mother the shortest length of time and just how short that is."

When the bell rang for lunch, I went to the dictionary, but I was not looking up animals. I looked up the word *embargo.* It said: *An order of a government prohibiting the departure of commercial ships from its ports.* Rosalind was right. I really was a blunderbuss.

All the time we were eating in the lunchroom, we talked about Mr. Dooley's baby.

"I'll bet when Mrs. Dooley goes to the hospital, he'll miss a whole lot of school," said Jody.

Sara opened her lunch sack. She had a hard-boiled egg. "Once I cracked open an egg and there was blood in the yolk," she told us.

"Euuuw!" said Jody and Dawn together.

"That means if the hen had kept sitting on it, it would have turned into a chicken," said Sara.

We thought about that for a while.

"That's all a hen has to do? Lay an egg and sit on it, and it turns into a chicken?" I asked.

"I guess," said Sara. She asked if I wanted to trade my cheese sandwich for her hard-boiled egg, and I said no. After that nobody wanted her egg.

"How does a baby grow inside its mother without eating anything?" asked Megan.

"It eats," said Rosalind. "I think it eats its mother."

"Rosalind!" I said.

"Just the lining of her stomach or something," Rosalind said.

I knew that couldn't be right. A baby isn't in its mother's stomach anyway.

"If a baby eats inside its mother, where does it go to the bathroom?" asked Dawn. We looked at each other.

"Inside its mother!" we all said together.

"Euuuw!" Dawn and Jody squealed.

We were glad there weren't any babies growing inside of us.

When we came in off the playground after lunch, Mr. Dooley was tipped back in his chair, his head against the blackboard. His eyes were closed. He jumped when he heard us coming and pretended he hadn't been asleep at all.

We had our history and geography lessons, but just before we went home, Rosalind raised her hand. "Does a baby eat when it's inside its mother?" she asked.

"Yes, but not the same way we eat," said Mr. Dooley. "It's attached to its mother by an umbilical cord—I'll be showing you pictures of that later—and its nourishment comes through that cord. Sort of like a feeding tube, you might say."

We looked at each other, wondering who was going to ask the gross question.

"Well," said Sara, "if it eats inside its mother, where does it . . . ?"

But Mr. Dooley knew what she was going to ask. "Poop and pee?" he said, and we all laughed out loud. "Well, by the fifth month the fetus begins to urinate—to pee—inside its mother's womb, that special place where the baby grows. But the urine's sterile, so it doesn't do any harm. As for poop, that's called meconium. It stays inside the baby and comes out after it's born. As our baby gets bigger, I'll tell you lots more.

The whole story of how a baby grows inside its mother is really quite remarkable!"

"*I* think it's remarkably messy!" said Rosalind, and we all laughed again. That's what I like most about my two best friends. They always make me laugh.

At dinner that night I said, "Guess what? Mr. Dooley is having a baby!"

"Well, *that* should make medical history," said Lester.

"His *wife,* Lester. I mean, he and his wife are expecting a baby. And that's why he was late to school this morning. His wife isn't sleeping so well and neither is he."

"Ah, yes," said Dad. "I remember those early months."

I was staring down at my lima beans, thinking about the things Mr. Dooley had drawn on the blackboard. About an elephant carrying a baby for 660 days. "Do I have to have a baby when I grow up?" I asked.

"No," said Dad. "Not if you don't want to. And you don't have to decide it right now, either."

"But do I have to have a baby if I get married?"

"Nope. You and your husband can decide that together."

"Maybe I won't want any kids, or maybe I'll just adopt a lot of orphans," I told him.

"You could do that, too," said Dad.

I was still fooling around with my lima beans when Dad and Lester started their dessert.

"How come *women* have to have all the babies? Why can't men have some of them?" I asked.

"Ouch!" said Lester.

"Because men's bodies weren't made for babies, Alice. You know that. We couldn't grow a baby if we tried," said Dad.

"No fair!" I complained. "I wish I'd been a boy. I wish I could be a man."

"No, you don't," said Lester.

"Why not?"

"You'd have to shave your face every day or grow a beard."

"That wouldn't be so bad," I said.

"You'd have to play football . . ."

"Now, Lester," said Dad.

"And be in the army . . ."

"So what?" I said. "I'll bet having a baby hurts."

"It hurts some, but it didn't stop your mother from wanting another baby after she'd had Lester," said Dad. "She wanted you very much, Alice. And besides, doctors know how to keep it from hurting too much."

"Yep, after Mom had me, she thought I was so wonderful, she wanted another just like me. And what did she get? You!" said Lester. And that *you* sounded just like *yuck*.

• • •

I went to our encyclopedias after dinner and looked up *animals*. I found the section on birth. Just like Mr. Dooley said, elephants keep their babies inside them the longest. And it said that opossums keep their babies in them the shortest time—only twelve days.

I called Rosalind and told her about the opossums. I asked her how she would like to carry a baby around inside of her for 660 days. Rosalind didn't even want to carry a baby for nine months.

"We wouldn't have to have human babies," said Rosalind. "You could work at a zoo with me, and we could take care of animal babies."

That seemed like a good idea. But, as Dad said, I didn't have to decide that right away either.

8

The List

The next time the Naked Nomads came over to practice, Rosalind came along with her brother, so I invited Sara for the afternoon too. Lester doesn't want me around when his friends come by. He tries to pretend he doesn't have any sister at all. I'll bet if Lester had his choice between me and a new car, he'd be driving a Mustang this very minute.

Dad was in his room with the door closed, trying to order Christmas presents from a catalog. It was hard to find any place in the house to get away from the noise in the basement.

Rosalind and Sara and I were sprawled across my bed, where Oatmeal was asleep on my pillow. We were looking at old-fashioned paper dolls that Sara had brought over. There were four paper dolls of women of the 1800s, all wearing old-fashioned underwear—long bloomers down below their knees and corsets that squeezed their waists so tight, I'll bet their stomachs rumbled all the time.

There were paper dresses to fasten on them that reached their ankles and big bonnets and lacy shawls.

"I'm glad we don't have to wear all this stuff," I said, fastening a cape over a woman in a ruffled dress. "I would probably trip and break my legs."

"I'll bet your great-grandmother dressed like this," said Rosalind.

"Your great-great-*great*-grandma, maybe," said Sara. She was putting different hats on the paper dolls and tried out a hat with ostrich feathers that hung down over the doll's eyes. She looked at me. "Are you ever going to get another mom?" she asked.

I shrugged. "I'll bet there are a lot of women who would marry my dad if I asked them. I just can't think of anyone I'd *want* to be my mother."

"What you need is a list," said Rosalind.

"Of people?"

"Of what you want a new mother to be like," Rosalind explained.

"You mean, sort of like ordering from a catalog?" I asked.

"No. If your dad ever tells you he wants to marry again, then you can give him your list," Rosalind said.

So we put the paper dolls away, and I got out my yellow notebook from school. On one side of the top sheet I wrote *yes,* and on the other side I wrote *no.*

"What shall I write in the *yes* column?" I asked.

"Write down *kind,*" said Sara.

I wrote *kind.*

"Good cook," said Rosalind.

I wrote that, too.

"Smart," said Sara.

"Doesn't snore," said Rosalind. We giggled.

"Funny," said Sara. "Sexy." We laughed some more.

"What shall I write under *no*?" I asked.

"Picks her nose," said Rosalind.

"Yells a lot," said Sara.

"Cooks squash and spinach," said Rosalind.

"Won't help with your homework," I said, and wrote it down.

"Bad breath," said Rosalind.

"Rotten teeth."

"Cruel."

"If your dad ever marries again, Alice," said Rosalind, "you'd better make him sign a paper that says he won't marry any woman on your *no* list."

"If he does, you'll be stuck with her forever," said Sara.

After the Naked Nomads had gone home and Rosalind and Sara had left too, I lay on my bed, Oatmeal purring on my chest, and stared at a crack in the ceiling. I don't like friends to ask about my mother. It makes me feel different from everyone else. I think they expect me to cry.

Sometimes I do cry a little bit when I'm alone. I wish I remembered her better. I don't remember being a baby at all. I can't remember her rocking me or nursing me or kissing the top of my head, so I don't know if I'm crying because I miss *her* or because I miss having any mother at all.

Dad came out of his bedroom, and I followed him to the kitchen. He says his ears always ring after the Naked Nomads go home.

"Are you ever going to marry again?" I asked.

He pulled out a pan to start supper. "I'd like to someday, but I don't have any prospects at the moment," he said. He looked at me sort of funny. "Why? Do you have any suggestions?"

I pushed my list toward him. Dad read down the *yes* and *no* columns.

"Ah! A checklist!" said Dad. "Well, a woman might have a checklist of her own, you know."

"What?"

"She might not want to marry a man who has children. Or she might want a man with a big house. Or she might not want a husband with any gray in his hair. All kinds of things."

I never thought of that. I didn't think that there was any woman in the world who wouldn't want to marry my dad.

He got out some meat and started making stew. "She may want to travel, she may hate to cook, she may want a man who will do all the housework, and she may especially hate mess and confusion and . . ."

Lester walked in the kitchen just then, still holding his drumsticks.

". . . noise," Dad said.

"Say what?" said Lester.

"Al and I were just talking about what a future wife for me ought to be like, and I was explaining that she may have some ideas of her own," said Dad.

Lester took out the orange juice, started to drink it right from the carton, then caught Dad's look and poured some in a glass instead. "Got anybody in mind?" he asked.

"Not at the moment."

"Not the mouth next door, I hope."

"Definitely not Mrs. Sheavers," said Dad.

"What about the one from your store?" asked Lester. "The severe-looking dame in sheet music."

"No. Janice Sherman is just a good friend."

"You oughta get out more, Dad. Go to the right clubs. Hang out at the beach in summer. Go where the babes go," said Lester.

"What 'babes' would those be, Lester?"

"Well, I guess I don't know where you'd find women your age," Lester said.

"Not the bars or the beach, that's for sure," Dad said, smiling a little. "But while I appreciate your suggestions, guys, it's really up to me. Okay?"

"Okay," I said.

"Okay by me," said Lester. "Just let me know before a decision's final."

"Of course," said Dad.

My list got me thinking, though, of the kind of person *I* want to be when I grow up. *I* want to be funny and smart and kind. How could you make sure you were going to grow up right unless you had somebody to copy? I thought of all the grown women I knew: Aunt Sally; my cousin Carol, who was *almost* a grown woman; Mrs. Sheavers; Janice Sherman; some of my old teachers. There wasn't anyone I wanted to be exactly like.

At school the next day I told Rosalind how I was having trouble finding a woman who was perfect.

"That's why I want to work with animals," said Rosalind.

"Animals are perfect?"

"No. But they don't make fun of you. They don't talk about you behind your back and say you can't eat with them at lunch."

That was true. "Is that why you want to work in the elephant house at the zoo?" I asked her.

"Nobody makes fun of an elephant. Not if they know what's good for them," she said.

I was thinking about what Mr. Dooley told us about elephants. "What do you suppose would happen if it was time for a baby elephant to be born and it didn't want to come out?" I said.

We thought about that for a minute.

"Maybe when a baby is ripe, it just falls out," said Rosalind. "Maybe if you don't go to the hospital when it's time, the baby will slide out when you're at the store or something. Maybe you would go to eat at McDonald's, and suddenly . . . whoops! There's a baby coming out!" She made a face. "Let's don't ever get married," she said.

"Let's just live in a big house together—you and me and Sara—and don't ever have husbands," I said. "Let's just have a big farm and raise orphans and stray dogs and cats."

"And elephants," said Rosalind.

"Okay. We'll have elephants, too," I told her.

9

Christmas for Three

I don't remember any Christmas when there weren't a lot of people around, but this was going to be the one.

"Christmas for three!" Dad said brightly, trying to let Lester and me know that it could still be a nice Christmas without Aunt Sally and Uncle Milt and Carol.

"Christmas for four!" I said. "We have Oatmeal, remember?" Our gray-and-white kitten hadn't celebrated a Christmas yet.

"Just keep her away from crinkle ribbon," said Dad. "Cats will eat anything."

"Even ribbon?" I asked.

"Ha!" said Lester. "Haven't you ever seen a cat with one end of a ribbon sticking out its mouth and the other end sticking out its rear?"

"Lester, that's gross!" I said.

"Cats are gross," said Lester. My brother isn't exactly fond of cats. What *I* think he is fond of is the girl named Lisa.

He says she's just a friend from history class, but I saw her name, *Lisa Shane,* scribbled in pencil on the back of our phone book, along with her telephone number. I saw the initials *LS* written in four different directions on the cover of Lester's three-ring notebook. One night when he was talking to her on the phone, he was doodling on the telephone pad, and when I looked at it later, I saw that he had drawn pairs of eyes with eyelashes all over the notepad and had written *Lisalisalisalisalisa* all over the place. If that's not love, what is it?

One night Lester and I were doing the dishes, and I said, "Lisa's your girlfriend, isn't she?"

"No," said Lester. "Just a friend."

"Ha!" I said. "You've got her name on everything! I don't see Mickey Larson's name on everything."

"I'm just being nice to a girl who needs a friend," said Lester.

I took the dish he handed me and wiped it dry. When Lester and I do the dishes together, we don't use the dishwasher because then we won't have to empty it later.

"Why does she need friends so bad?" I asked.

"Well," said Lester, "she's an orphan, and she was adopted by this really mean couple. They make her work day and night, and only give her scraps of food from the table. They didn't want a daughter, they just wanted a servant. She cries herself to sleep."

I looked at Lester. "Is this really true?"

"Of course!"

"Why doesn't she run away?" I asked.

"Where would she go?" asked Lester.

"She could come and live with us."

Lester shook his head. "They'd never let her."

"So how can you help?" I asked.

"Oh, I buy her things and talk to her. She's saving up enough money for a plane ticket. Then she's going someplace they'll never find her. China, I think."

That was a really sad story, and I was proud of my brother for wanting to help Lisa Shane. "Her parents don't beat her, do they?"

"Every night," said Lester.

"She should *tell* somebody!" I said.

"Her father would beat her all the harder if she did. That's why she wants to go to Japan."

"I thought you said China."

"Right. China . . . Japan. It doesn't make any difference."

"What would she do there, Lester?" I asked.

"Oh, she wants to help out people who work in rice

paddies. She's got a heart of gold," he said. "I'm just trying to be her friend and help her save enough money to buy a plane ticket."

I wished we could invite her over here, but Lester said her adoptive parents wouldn't let her. No, he just has to be the best friend he can, but he can't help worrying about her.

It was really sad about Lisa Shane, but I decided I wouldn't let anything ruin Christmas. Just like Dad said, it would be a cozy little Christmas for three. Four, counting Oatmeal.

The week before Christmas everyone is excited and fidgety at school, even people who don't celebrate Christmas. Jody and Ollie are Jewish, so they don't have Christmas at their houses, but they get the same vacation we do.

"What do you do on Christmas?" I asked Jody.

"Go to the movies," she said. "We have a big break-fast at Grandma and Grandpa's, and then all of our aunts and uncles and cousins go to the movies. And it's never crowded."

Mr. Dooley was excited too. He said that his wife thought maybe she had felt their baby move around inside her that morning, and it's always a big moment when a baby starts to kick.

"Does it hurt?" Sara wanted to know.

"No. It's more like a little flutter," said Mr. Dooley.

"My wife says it feels like a butterfly batting its wings inside her."

Somehow I liked the idea of a baby inside me more than I liked the idea of a butterfly flying around, flapping its wings and trying to get out. I looked at Rosalind. She was looking at me. We were *definitely* not going to have babies when we grew up. No butterfly babies for us!

Dad came home with a huge Christmas tree. It smelled as though it had been freshly cut and was one of the biggest trees I'd ever seen. It was so tall, we had to saw off some of the trunk so it wouldn't scrape the ceiling.

"Just because there's only three of us doesn't mean we can't have a big tree," said Dad.

"Way to go, Pop!" said Lester.

We had two strings of lights, but they covered only half the tree, so Lester strung them all in front where we could see them. We didn't have nearly enough ornaments, either.

"Are we poor, Dad?" I asked, gently lifting out the angel that went at the top of the tree.

"We're not exactly rich," he answered. "Music stores don't pay their employees a whole lot of money, but it's work I love to do. Why?"

"Everything we have is old."

"That's because I figured it would cost more to move

our furniture from Chicago to Takoma Park than it would to just sell it and buy some used furniture here. We're just average, Alice. Not rich, not poor. We're in-between."

I thought about that a minute. "I know!" I said. "Why don't I have a Christmas party and invite some friends to come over and make ornaments for our tree!"

"Great idea!" said Dad. "Friday night would be the best for me."

"The Naked Nomads are coming over to practice then," said Lester. "The mall wants amateur groups to come by and play Christmas carols on Saturday. We're scheduled from ten thirty in the morning to eleven."

"Christmas carols? The Naked Nomads?" said Dad in surprise. "Well, Alice, I guess you'll have live music for your party, then, won't you?"

I didn't invite any boys. I didn't want to even *think* about having to marry any of the boys in my class when I was grown up, even though Donald Sheavers was supposed to be my boyfriend.

So Megan and Dawn and Jody and Rosalind and Sara all came over after dinner on Friday to help decorate our tree.

"It's such a big tree, we sort of ran out of stuff," I said.

"Popcorn!" said Rosalind, who always thinks of food first. "If you have a big needle and a long piece of thread and some popcorn, we could string that to go on the tree."

Dad was in the dining room addressing Christmas cards. "I'll make the popcorn," he said. "And let me look for some needles and thread."

"We could use foil wrap to make stars," said Jody.

"Foil wrap coming up," said Dad.

I found some old Barbie doll dresses with spangles on them. We cut them into pieces to wrap around acorns from my collection, and then we tucked those among the branches of the tree.

The Naked Nomads came over around eight thirty. Pretty soon we heard them tuning up in the basement.

"That's 'O Little Town of Bethlehem,'" Dad said, surprised, I guess, that he could actually recognize something.

While Rosalind and Dawn were stringing popcorn and Jody was making foil stars, Sara and Megan and I went into my room to see if we could find anything else to go on the tree. We found a red Barbie doll shoe, a purple glass necklace, a gold-colored ring, and some seashells.

"It's a very unusual-looking tree," said Dawn. "All it needs now is a paper-clip chain."

So we made a paper-clip chain. After that we put all my bracelets on the branches, and then we dangled some old cuff links of Dad's from the highest branch.

Dad even took a picture when we were through.

But it was sad thinking how much fun we were hav-ing and what a hard life Lester's friend Lisa Shane had. So when we took a break and went to my room, I closed the door behind me and told my five friends that I had a secret. But I couldn't tell them, I said, unless they promised me on their word of honor they would never, ever tell.

Rosalind, who was opening and closing my dresser drawers, turned around, and her mouth fell open. "What?" she said.

"I can't tell unless you *promise* you will never give away this secret, because if you do, something horrible will happen," I said.

"We promise," everybody said together.

But that wasn't enough. I put my hand on my dresser and made Sara put her hand on top of mine, then Megan's on top of Sara's, until all twelve of our hands were piled one on top of the other. Everyone's eyes were on me. Sara's nose was stuffed up, and we were so quiet that I could even hear her breathing through her mouth.

"If you ever tell what I'm going to tell you, a girl will be beaten black and blue," I said.

I think Jody and Dawn stopped breathing.

"We *promise* promise!" Megan said.

We all climbed up on my bed and sat in a circle. I told them about Lisa Shane—how she was beaten and half starved by her adoptive parents and how Lester was secretly helping her save enough money to go to China.

"What's she going to do in China?" asked Dawn.

"Work in a rice paddy," I said.

"Why doesn't she go to Paris or someplace?" asked Megan. "If I were going to run away, I wouldn't go to a rice paddy."

"Because she loves other people and knows what it's like to be poor," I said.

"*We* could help her!" said Sara. "We could each save up a little bit of money and maybe send it to her as a present!"

"That's what I was thinking," I said.

"Maybe we could put some food in it too," said Rosalind.

"Does she have enough clothes?" asked Dawn.

"I'll bet she only wears clothes with long sleeves so no one can see the bruises," said Jody.

"When should we send her the stuff?" asked Rosalind.

"Why don't we wait till we've collected twenty dollars, and then we'll put everything in a box and mail it," I told them. "But we can't let *any*one know. It's just our secret."

"We'll be the Secret Six!" said Rosalind.

We all put our hands together again, one on top of the other, and said that if any of us ever told Lisa

Shane's secret, may all the trees in a forest fall on that person's head.

We went back out in the living room. The Naked Nomads had been practicing for an hour, and Lester came upstairs to ask Dad how they sounded. I saw all the girls look at Lester sorrowfully.

"Sounds pretty cool to me," Dad said. "A little less saxophone on 'Silent Night,' and I think you could do a bit more with the drum on 'We Three Kings.' Use the wood block, maybe—like horses' hooves, you know?"

"Camels," I said.

"Whatever," said Lester.

Dad got out the ice cream then, a half gallon of chocolate chunk and a half gallon of Rocky Road, and made hot-fudge sauce so we could have sundaes. Everyone, even the Naked Nomads, sat around the living room eating hot-fudge sundaes and taking turns dragging a long string with popcorn on the end for Oatmeal to chase.

"I wish we could share this ice cream with Lisa Shane," Megan whispered.

"Me too," I told her.

When everyone had gone home, Lester and I turned out all the lights except the ones on the tree, and then the three of us sat down together to admire it. It was still sort of bare in places, but it was *our* tree.

"It looks like bargain day at the five-and-ten," Lester said.

"I think it's beautiful," I told him. I turned to Dad. "Would Mom have liked this tree?"

"She would have loved it. She liked to make things out of nothing," Dad said.

Lester put his hands behind his head, stretched out his legs, and studied the tree some more. All three of us were quiet for a while.

"I miss having a mom at Christmas," I said finally in a small voice.

"I miss Marie all the time," said Dad. "But especially at Christmas. She loved to give homemade presents. Les, do you remember when we built a wagon for you out of an old apple box and some wheels? It was about the ugliest thing I ever saw, but Marie gave you some spray paint, and you made a royal mess."

"I don't remember the wagon very well, but I remember the paint," Lester said. "I painted it blue first, and then I made zigzag lines in yellow, and they all turned green. I couldn't figure it out."

We laughed.

"What else did we do when Mom was alive?" I asked.

"Well, let's see." Dad had his arm around me, and he patted my shoulder. "Your mother was crazy about snow. Once she got you and Lester up at midnight because there had been a beautiful snowfall. We put you both on a sled and pulled you around the neighborhood in the dark."

"I don't remember that," I said.

"*I* do," said Lester. "You were only a baby, and they had you sit between my legs. I was afraid you'd fall off and I'd get blamed for it."

"Did I?" I asked.

"Yes," said Dad, raising one eyebrow at Lester.

Lester grinned. "I just wanted her to get her first taste of the white stuff."

"Face-first," said Dad. "That was the giveaway. One minute she was snug between your legs, and the next she was spread-eagled facedown in the snow."

"Lester, how *could* you?" I laughed, turning on him and pounding his arm.

"You didn't even cry," he said. "You loved it."

I curled up against Dad again. "What else?"

"Well, your mother loved to do spur-of-the-moment things. Some summer nights I'd come home from work and she'd have a picnic basket all packed and waiting for me, a blanket under her arm. 'Where are we going?' I'd ask, and she'd say, 'Out in the back-yard.' And that's where we'd have a picnic."

"I wish *I* had more memories of her." I sighed. "I wish I had a lot of good things to remember."

"So do I," said Dad. "Small children forget most of what happens those first few years, honey. All I can tell you is that there *were* good times and that your mother loved you both very much."

And that, I guessed, would have to do.

. . .

We had a good Christmas under our special tree. I found a long plastic snake hanging out of my stocking—Lester *always* puts weird things in my stocking—but that was okay because I put a wishbone in his. I'd saved it from the turkey we had at Thanksgiving. Lester and I each took hold of one end of the wishbone and pulled. Lester got the biggest piece, which meant I was supposed to tell what I wished because *my* wish wasn't supposed to come true.

But I wouldn't tell, and Dad said I didn't have to. I'd wished that Lisa Shane would get to China so her parents would never find her. And I was going to help her get there because I didn't really believe in wishbones.

Dad and Lester liked my presents, though—a good-smelling deodorant stick for Lester and a crossword puzzle book for Dad. I liked my gifts from them, too—a pink sweater with colored stripes on it and a pair of sunglasses with sparkles around the frame and a book about Egyptian mummies and some gold and silver pens.

Uncle Harold and Uncle Howard called from Tennessee to wish us Merry Christmas, and Aunt Sally sent me a dress and some thong beach sandals that were way too big.

It's all right, I thought when I tried on the sandals. *I'll put them in the box for Lisa Shane.*

❀ ❀ 10 ❀ ❀

Trouble

My dad says that nobody can get you in trouble but yourself. So when Rosalind got me in trouble one day in January, I could have said no. The problem was, it didn't sound like trouble at the time, it sounded like fun.

There had been a really wild winter storm with high winds on Wednesday. We got two feet of snow. The schools were closed for the rest of the week, and Rosalind came over on Thursday. That's when it happened.

There's a chain-link fence around our backyard, and a neighbor's garage backs right up to it. The snow in one corner had piled up against the fence and garage so high that it was way over our heads. Lester was in charge that day. He said Rosalind and I could play outside, so that's what we did.

We decided to make a cave in that big snowdrift. The snow was packed so hard that when we dug out handfuls from the bottom, it stayed all packed around the hole.

"This is really going to be good," said Rosalind. "If we pour water on it before I go home, it will freeze into an ice house."

We dug so long that I had to go in the house for extra mittens.

"Wha'cha doing out there?" Lester said, coming into the kitchen in his stocking feet.

"Making a snow cave," I said. "When we get it done, I'll bet even you could fit inside it, Lester!"

"Yeah? I'll come out and look at it when you're finished," said Lester.

When I went back out, Rosalind said why didn't we dig just a little bit more and then go get something to eat.

"Let's just keep digging till we can both fit inside. We've got to dig a lot farther back," I said. We dug some more.

"I'm hungry," Rosalind complained finally. "What can we eat?"

"I don't know," I said. "Dad's at work and Lester's in charge. What do you want?"

"Do you have any bread?" asked Rosalind.

"I think so."

"Do you have any butter?"

"Yes."

"Cheese?"

"Uh-huh."

"Pickles?"

"Yes."

"How about a grilled cheese sandwich and a Coke," said Rosalind.

"Okay," I said. "As soon as we finish our snow cave."

We dug a few minutes longer, and then we both crawled in. I crawled way to the back so there would still be room for Rosalind, but it was a tight squeeze. I wanted it to be wide enough for us to sit facing each other with our legs crossed so we could tell ghost stories or something.

"I'm *really* hungry," said Rosalind, and she crawled back out again. She lowered her head so she could see me at the very back of our cave.

"Okay," I said. "Lester will make some sandwiches for us. Let's just dig out a few more inches on both sides back here." I stayed inside and looked around. "It could probably be a few inches higher, too, so we wouldn't have to keep our heads down."

"You know what?" said Rosalind, beginning to smile. She was sitting on the ground outside with her legs out in front of her. "You know what we could do? We could pretend you got buried in a cave-in, and I'll scream and Lester will come running out of the house."

"No!" I said. "I want to save it."

"It would be fun. Lester would freak out."

"He never freaks out."

"Let's do it just to see what happens," Rosalind said. And before I could answer, Rosalind leaned back, bracing herself on her hands, and kicked at the front of our snow cave. All the snow came down on top of me.

I had been sitting with my knees up to my chest, and as soon as I'd felt the snow coming down, I put my face on my knees, my nose between them. There was an empty space under my legs so I could still breathe, but snow was piled on top of my head and shoulders, and I didn't know snow could be so heavy.

I heard Rosalind scream just like she said she would, but it sounded like a real scream to me. I didn't know how much snow had come down, but it had been piled up almost as high as the roof on the windy side of our neighbor's garage. I was afraid that if I tried to crawl out and went the wrong way, I might not be able to breathe, so I stayed right where I was, with my nose stuck in the air pocket under my knees.

Now I really *was* scared.

Then I heard a door slam. Somebody else was screaming. Was that Mrs. Sheavers? Another door banged.

I couldn't make out what anyone was saying, but I

could hear a louder voice now that sounded like Lester's. I could feel the thud of feet on the ground, like someone running. Then the sound of scraping, like people digging.

Lester would bawl me out, I knew. He would ask why I didn't just crawl out, but he didn't know how heavy the snow was on my neck.

Someone touched me. Someone yelled. More hands were digging now, because they poked at me. I couldn't let Lester find me this way—sitting here perfectly alive! So I closed my eyes and slumped over as a hand grabbed my arm.

"I've got her! I've found her!" I heard Lester yell, and his voice was shaky.

I heard Rosalind sob. A *real* sob, I thought. Mrs. Sheavers screamed again. She sounded like a siren.

Lester pulled me out and stretched me out on the ground, brushing snow from my face, his breath coming in fast little pants.

"Is she breathing?" cried Mrs. Sheavers.

"She's breathing," said Lester. Was he about to cry? I opened one eye to see, and I saw Donald Sheavers looking down at me like I was an exhibit in a museum. I sat up.

"She's okay!" cried Rosalind, clapping her hands.

"Oh, thank heaven!" gasped Donald's mother.

"Al!" Lester said. "What happened?"

"The snow fell in on her," said Rosalind.

"We saved her!" cried Mrs. Sheavers. "I was never so scared! Don't you girls know any better than to dig in a snowbank like that?"

I looked at Rosalind. She looked at me. I had snow all down my neck and up the cuffs of my sleeves.

Mrs. Sheavers went back in her house, and Lester took me by the arm. "Al, come on in and get dry clothes," he said, and I knew for sure he would trade me for a car if he could.

"I'm going home, Alice," said Rosalind. "I don't want any lunch."

"Yeah, you do that," said Lester.

I went inside and shook out my clothes. Snow fell all over the floor. I draped my jacket and mittens and cap over the kitchen chairs and went back in my bedroom. I tracked snow onto the round rug beside my bed. My hair was wet. There was still snow on my eyelashes. I had just pulled on a clean T-shirt and some dry socks when I heard a car door slam and Dad came hurrying through the front door.

"Al?" he called. "Lester? What happened?"

How did he *find out so soon?* I wondered.

"She's okay," Lester said. "The snow caved in on her, that's all."

"Mrs. Sheavers called me at the store and said she helped rescue Alice from a cave-in. What's going on?"

He could see that I was perfectly all right.

"I'm fine," I said, but I felt awful. Awful for the fuss we had caused. Awful because of what Rosalind did. Awful because maybe I should have crawled out and not got Mrs. Sheavers all upset. Awful because our snow cave was ruined. I started to cry.

Lester turned on me. "What are you crying about? You're fine!" he said.

But Dad turned on Lester. "Les, where were *you* when all this was going on? Didn't you know the girls were digging a cave back there?"

"Dad, I didn't think it was dangerous! I've made a dozen snow caves, and nobody ever worried about me! I still can't believe she couldn't have just crawled out."

"I was afraid to move," I said. "I wanted to keep my nose between my knees where I could still breathe."

"That was smart thinking, Al," said Dad. "I'm glad you used your head. But that was dangerous!" He turned on Lester again. "Les, you have to be responsible!" he said. "When you're in charge, I don't want to be worrying if you're reliable or not. When I get a call like that from Mrs. Sheavers, what am I supposed to think?"

"That she's as nutty as a fruitcake," Lester growled. "About the only thing Mrs. Sheavers did was stand there and scream."

Dad turned back to me. "Didn't you stop to think

that the snow might come down on top of you?"

"Well, it wouldn't have if Rosalind hadn't—" I stopped.

"Wouldn't have what?" asked Lester, fixing his eyes on me.

"Wouldn't have . . . kicked . . . at it . . . just to see what would happen," I finished. There wasn't anything else to do but tell the whole story.

"You mean she caved that in on purpose?" Lester yelled.

"She did it before I could stop her!" I said miserably.

"*Why?*" asked Dad.

"Rosalind said . . . said . . . wouldn't it be funny . . . if I was buried in the snow and she'd scream and . . ."

"Alice Kathleen McKinley!" Dad exploded. "Do you mean this was all a big joke?"

"I didn't know she was going to kick our cave in! I didn't know she meant it!" I said.

Dad shook his head disgustedly. "Well, this sure put a dent in my afternoon," he said. "Do you think possibly I could go back to work and finish out the day without anything else happening?"

We both mumbled that he could. Dad left the house again. Lester shot me an angry look as he went downstairs to the basement, and I crept off to my room. It would be a long time, I knew, before he would make a grilled cheese sandwich for Rosalind.

11

The Valentine Blunder

"Well, if I'm a blunderbuss, you're a bigger one," I said to Rosalind on Monday. "You really got me in trouble. Dad and Lester are mad at me, and Mrs. Sheavers is going around telling everyone how she and Donald saved my life."

"I didn't think she'd call your dad," said Rosalind.

"You didn't think about anything!" I said, sounding exactly like him. "Besides, I really *could* have smothered if I hadn't stuck my nose between my knees."

Somehow that sounded funny, and we laughed in spite of ourselves, but I was still a little mad at Rosalind for kicking down our snow cave. Dad had forgiven me soon enough, because he really loves me. What I felt worst about, though, was Lester being mad at me. I wished I could tell him what the

Secret Six were going to do for Lisa Shane.

At recess Donald went around telling everyone how I almost got buried alive. Then Rosalind got in on the act, and everyone got so interested, I decided I might as well enjoy telling *my* part of the story.

"How could you breathe with all that snow on top of you?" Dawn asked.

"It wasn't easy," I said.

"Could you hear them digging for you?"

"A little."

"Couldn't you just dig your way out?" asked Ollie.

"It was hard to tell which end was up," I said, which wasn't exactly true.

Mr. Dooley, of course, turned it into a science lesson when he heard about it. He gave us a little talk about how digging in snow or sand or mud could be dangerous. But somehow the conversation got back to his baby, and this time he'd brought in a sonogram to show us.

At first we couldn't make out what we were seeing. It's not like a photograph. It's all black and white, and the fetus looked more like a squirrel or a gopher with an enormous head than a baby, but Mr. Dooley pointed out its fist and we could even see the thumb.

"And now we know what it's going to be. A little boy," he said.

"How do you know?" asked Megan.

Everyone waited, grinning. Someone even laughed. Even I knew the answer to that one.

"Because of this little thing right down there," said Mr. Dooley, pointing to a tiny fingerlike thing between the baby's legs.

Megan stared hard at the sonogram, and I remembered that she didn't have any brothers. Even girls with brothers as private as Lester is about his body see them naked once or twice.

"That's a penis," said Mr. Dooley. "That's how you tell a boy from a girl." Then he went on to tell us what a fetus looks like when it's been growing inside its mother for six months. "By now," he said, "hair is growing on his head, and he can kick and even hiccup."

We laughed.

"What's his name?" asked Ollie.

"Oh, we haven't got that far yet," said Mr. Dooley, smiling. "For now he's just Baby Dooley."

When we had afternoon recess, I told the other girls in the Secret Six to meet me over by the fence. We needed to see how much money we had so far to send Lisa Shane to China. We figured we had saved nine dollars and seventy-three cents.

"How do you know she's really going to go to

China?" Jody asked. "How do you know she won't go out and buy a sweater?"

"It will be either China or Japan," I told her solemnly. "She wants to go clear across the world so her adoptive parents will never find her."

I wondered, though, if maybe Lester was fibbing about China. Maybe Lisa wasn't interested in the Chinese at all. When I came in the house that afternoon, though, he was talking to Lisa Shane on the phone. I can always tell if it's Lisa because he smiles all the while he's talking to her.

"You don't eat enough to keep a dog alive . . . ," he was saying. I sat down across the room and pretended I was reading the comics. There were long pauses when Lisa must have been doing the talking. "You did not," said Lester. He smiled some more. "No, you didn't. I watched you. You ate half an apple and three rice cakes."

That was enough for me. Rice cakes . . . a rice paddy . . . Lester *had* to be telling the truth.

At dinner that night I looked at a piece of asparagus on my fork and said, "Mr. Dooley's baby has a penis."

"Ah! A boy!" said Dad.

"And just how did you find *that* out?" Lester asked me.

"He showed us a sonogram. You can see it in the picture."

"Man! You learn all kinds of stuff in school these days, don't you?" said Lester.

When Valentine's Day came around, we still hadn't collected twenty dollars for Lisa Shane. We were having a party at school, though, and the art teacher asked each of us to bring an old shoe box to school and decorate it. She had crepe paper and ribbon and stars and spangles and stickers and foil and glue that we could use. We were supposed to put our names on the lids and cut slots in them.

Mr. Dooley made a box too, with red, white, and blue stripes. Mr. Dooley is very patriotic. Sara says he'll probably call his baby George Washington Dooley or Abraham Lincoln Dooley.

For the Valentine's party we were supposed to drop cards in the boxes of our friends. If you gave one to a girl, though, you had to give one to all the girls. If you gave one to a boy, you had to give one to all the boys. I didn't want to give valentines to boys, so I didn't even give one to Donald, even though he's supposed to be my boyfriend.

I had made valentines for all the girls, but then I got this great idea. The Saturday before Valentine's Day, I decided that Lisa Shane would just have to wait to go to China. I went to the Melody Inn with Dad that morning and asked Loretta Jenkins what I could buy at the Gift Shoppe with one dollar for Mr. Dooley's baby. The Gift Shoppe has T-shirts and caps and scarves and coffee mugs and ties, and everything is connected to music. I thought maybe I could get something left over from our Beethoven's Birthday sale.

"How big is the baby?" asked Loretta.

"Seven months," I said. "But it's still inside Mrs. Dooley. It won't be born until April."

"Oh," she said. "That *is* a tiny baby, then. We don't have much for babies, but this is the tiniest thing I've got." She took out a box of knit stocking caps for newborn babies. There were pink ones and blue ones and yellow and white ones. And they all said HAPPY BIRTHDAY, BEETHOVEN on them. Beethoven, of course, is a composer, and I had just learned to pronounce it right: "*Bay*-toe-van." I used to call him "*Beet*-oven" till Lester told me how stupid that sounded.

I chose a blue cap with white letters. "Is a dollar and five cents enough?" I asked.

"It is with your dad's discount," Loretta said, and put it in a bag for me.

When I got home, I folded the little cap in half and put it inside a big valentine. On the envelope I wrote, *For Baby Dooley*. On Monday, I pushed it down inside Mr. Dooley's red, white, and blue box for our Valentine's Day party after lunch that afternoon. I *could* do the right thing sometimes. A *nice* thing. I *could* use my head. I wasn't a blunderbuss all the time.

I was so excited at the thought of Mr. Dooley opening my valentine that at lunchtime in the all-purpose room I told the other girls at my table.

"You *didn't*!" said Dawn.

I stared at her. "Of course I did!" I said.

"You're not supposed to buy presents for a baby until it's just about to be born, Alice!" she said.

"*Why?*" I cried.

"Because something might happen to it. If it dies before it's born, then the parents will be sad every time they look at your present," said Jody, as though *every*-one knew that.

Now the other girls were nodding. I didn't know that! How did other girls know when you could give presents to a baby and when you couldn't?

"You're supposed to wait and give presents at a baby shower," said Sara. "That's when you give presents to someone who isn't born yet."

I felt awful! Mr. Dooley was going to hate me. If anything happened to Baby Dooley, he would remember me forever as "the girl who gave a little cap to our dead baby."

I had to get it back!

"What am I going to *do*?" I asked the other girls.

"I'll go ask Mr. Dooley what kind of a tree is growing

outside our window, and when he goes to look, you take his box to the rest room and get your valentine out," said Sara.

When we went back inside after hurrying through our lunches, Sara said, "Mr. Dooley, what kind of tree is that outside our window?"

Mr. Dooley was sorting through some papers on his desk. "A maple, Sara," he said.

"Not the big tree. That smaller one," said Sara.

"Which one do you mean?" asked Mr. Dooley, and he walked over to the window with her. That's when I picked up Mr. Dooley's red, white, and blue box off the table at the back of the room and walked right out the door with it and down the hall to the girls' rest room.

When I got there, though, I discovered that Mr. Dooley hadn't wrapped the lid and the box separately so that you could just take off the lid. He had wrapped them both together in the same sheet of red, white, and blue paper, and there was no way to get the lid off without cutting through the paper. Then Mr. Dooley would know that someone had opened his box!

Maybe I could squeeze my hand inside, I thought. Maybe I could push my fingers through the slot and feel around for a thick envelope and pull it out. I went to the last stall in the rest room and stepped inside. Bracing the box against one knee, I tried to slide my fingers through the slot without stretching it. I could barely get them in. Other valentines had been shoved in on top of mine. I pushed until half my hand was in the box.

I could hear music coming from the classroom across the hall, and I knew that the third graders were having the music teacher that day in Mrs. Burstin's room. She was the teacher I had last year.

Suddenly Mrs. Burstin herself walked into the rest room and began washing her hands at the sink. I stepped back farther in the stall and tried to close the door with my elbow.

"Alice?" said Mrs. Burstin, coming down the row of toilets. And then she was staring at me, standing there in the last stall with my hand stuck in the lid of Mr. Dooley's valentine box.

I saw her eyes travel down to the box with Mr. Dooley's name in big black letters.

"Does your teacher know you're here?" she asked.

"N-No," I said, and my cheeks felt as red as valentine candy.

Mrs. Burstin studied me. "What's the matter, Alice?"

"I'm trying to take back the valentine I gave to Mr. Dooley," I said, and my chin trembled.

"Oh. You wrote something on it you wish you hadn't?" she asked.

"No. It's for his fetus, and it might make him sad if

it dies," I said, swallowing. "I didn't know you weren't supposed to give presents to babies until just before they're born."

Mrs. Burstin reached down and helped me get my fingers out of the box. "You know what?" she said. "I think Mr. and Mrs. Dooley will be so pleased that you thought of a valentine for their baby that they will love it no matter what."

"Really?" I said.

"Really."

"But how am I going to get the box back in the room without anyone seeing?" I asked.

"I'll tell you what. Why don't you give it to me. I'll think of some reason to have Mr. Dooley called to the principal's office before your party starts, and as soon as he leaves the room, I'll pop in and return the box. He won't even know."

I handed the box to Mrs. Burstin. "Thank you," I said.

When I went back to my room, Mr. Dooley stopped talking for a moment because he hadn't realized I'd been gone. He waited until I sat down. Then he went on talking about how a human fetus has a tail at five weeks inside its mother, but at seven weeks the tail begins to shrink. I didn't know I had a tail once! That means Mr. Dooley once had a tail! Rosalind had a tail, and so did Dad and Lester!

"Where is it? The valentine?" whispered Jody.

"In the box," I whispered back.

She stared at me. "Where's the *box*?"

"Mrs. Burstin's got it," I said. "And she thinks the Dooleys will love my present no matter what."

12

Big Trouble

Mrs. Burstin was right; before I left for home that day, Mr. Dooley pulled me aside and told me it was one of the nicest valentines he had ever received.

It hadn't seemed like Valentine's Day because the week had been so warm that a lot of us took off our jackets at recess. When Donald Sheavers walked home with me after school, he gave me a chocolate marshmallow heart that looked as though he'd been carrying it around in his back pocket for a couple of days.

"You're supposed to give me something too if you're my girlfriend," said Donald.

Only a blunderbuss, I guess, would take a chocolate heart from her boyfriend on Valentine's Day and not give him anything. When we got to my house, I told him to wait on the steps. I went inside and asked Lester if we had any Snickers bars left from Halloween.

Lester went down in the basement and looked in his sock drawer. He found two. I took them out to Donald.

"Thanks," he said, and went home.

When I went back inside, Lester said, "How was the Valentine's party?"

"It was okay," I said. I sat down in my purple bean-bag chair and took the wrapper off the marshmallow heart. I ate all around the edge where the chocolate was until only the center was left.

"You want it?" I asked Lester. Lester will eat anything. He ate the marshmallow center.

"Where'd you get this?" he asked.

"Donald Sheavers."

"Ohhhh! Boyfriend?" he asked.

"I guess," I told him. Having a boyfriend was easy, easy, easy!

Lester licked his fingers. "Hey, Al," he said, "do me a favor?"

"What?"

"There's this girl at school . . ."

"Lisa Shane?" I asked. Lester looked surprised that I remembered her. "The girl who cries herself to sleep?"

"Oh, yeah. That's right! That's Lisa! Well, I'd sort of like to take her something tonight—maybe some valentine candy. Cheer her up." Lester actually sounded nice, like he wasn't mad at me anymore.

"Yeah?" I said.

"Well, you know how Dad is about me going out on school nights."

Of course I did. Dad goes to bed early, and whenever Lester goes out for the evening, school nights or not, Dad puts a big windup alarm clock outside his bedroom door. He sets the alarm for whenever Lester's supposed to be home. If Lester's not home in time to shut it off, the alarm goes off, Dad wakes up, and there's big trouble when Lester comes in.

"So?" I said.

"If I'm not home before ten twenty-five, will you turn off the alarm clock for me?" Lester asked.

"Les-ter!" I said. "I can't!"

"Just this once. Look. Lisa works at Borders, and she gets off at nine. I said I'd pick her up and drive her home. It will take fifteen minutes to get to her house and another fifteen to get back here by ten thirty."

"That leaves a whole hour to give her a box of candy, Lester," I said. It took Donald Sheavers four seconds to give me a chocolate marshmallow heart. Even in slow motion, I couldn't imagine it taking longer than four minutes to give a girl a box of candy. "So what do you need a whole hour for?" I asked. After all, he'd said she wasn't his girlfriend, so he didn't have to kiss her.

"I want to talk to her—see how she's doing. I'll look

like a nerd if I just give her some candy and tell her I have to go," Lester said.

"But how late *will* you be?"

"Not real late. I might even make it home before ten thirty. I just want you to stay up till ten twenty-five, and if I'm not home, go down the hall and turn off the alarm."

"Well, I'm only doing it this one time because it's Valentine's Day and I know how mean Lisa's parents treat her," I told him.

"You're the greatest," said Lester. "Just don't fall asleep. Okay?"

If I did this for Lester, maybe we could be real friends after all.

By the time Dad came home for dinner, Les and I had opened some canned salmon, mixed up some packaged mashed potatoes, and heated up frozen green beans. It was our night to cook. Dad, though, brought home a box of chocolates for our dessert that a customer had given him. I could tell by the way Lester looked at the box, tied with a gold ribbon, that he really wanted to trade the box he'd bought Lisa for this one, but he didn't dare. I was sure if we explained about Lisa and how her father beat her every night, Dad would let Lester have the best box. Lester wouldn't want me to say anything, though.

"Can I have the car a little while this evening, Dad?" he asked. "I promised to pick up a girl at Borders and drive her home."

"I thought you had a big physics test tomorrow."

"I do, but I've studied."

"Just be home by ten thirty," Dad said.

"Even on Valentine's Day?" asked Lester.

"Especially on Valentine's Day," Dad answered.

As soon as Lester left the house at a quarter of nine, I wished I hadn't promised to turn off the alarm. I was pretty miserable all evening, and when Dad found me still up, watching TV at nine thirty, he said, "Al, you were supposed to be in bed a half hour ago. Come on, get those PJs on."

"I'm not very sleepy," I said.

"You will be. Just climb in bed and your pillow will do the rest."

I stood up slowly, turned off the TV, and went down the hall to the bathroom. I took another five minutes to brush my teeth, then went in my room and checked my clock. Twenty of ten.

I heard Dad brushing his teeth. Then the soft thud of his footsteps back in his bedroom. There was the little *clunk* of the metal alarm clock as he set it on the floor outside his room.

"G'night, Al," he called.

"Good night, Dad." *Boy, Lester, you'd better come home and turn that alarm off yourself,* I thought. In a way it would be like lying to Dad, because I was making him think I was going to sleep when I wasn't.

I turned on my lamp and propped the pillows against the wall to keep me sitting up. The house was ghostly quiet. My ears felt as though they were going to pop off, I was listening so hard for our car. I looked at my clock. Ten of ten. I told myself I could only look at it every five minutes, so I counted to sixty five times, then looked. Nine fifty-five.

At ten o'clock Dad got up and went to the bathroom. I turned off my lamp. Dad went back to bed. I turned it on again.

What if the alarm went off a few minutes early? What if it went off at ten twenty-five, not ten thirty? I couldn't take any chances. At ten twenty-four, I tiptoed down the hall, felt around for the alarm button, and pushed it in.

Then I wrapped a blanket around me and went out to sit on the couch in the living room. Oatmeal was sleeping at the other end. She got up on her little cat feet, walked daintily across the cushions, and settled down in my lap.

What if Lester had been in an accident? If Lester didn't come home and the alarm went off, Dad would probably check with the police or call some hospitals to see if anyone had been brought in. Now the alarm wouldn't go off and Dad wouldn't even know that Lester was still out. Maybe Lester was lying by the side of the road this very minute with a broken neck! Maybe he was lying there hoping I hadn't turned the alarm off so that Dad would start looking for him.

I pulled the blanket up to my chin and leaned back against the cushions. Then I had another thought: Maybe he wasn't in an accident. Maybe Lisa Shane's father saw Lisa out in the car with Lester and tried to beat him up. I was worried, but not worried enough, I guess, because the darkness of the room, the softness of the blanket, and the warmth of my cat put me to sleep.

"Al?"

I tried to open my eyes, but I was too tired. I tried to pull myself out of my dream, but I kept drifting back.

"Al!" the voice said again, louder.

I forced my eyes open. There was a light on in the hallway, and I could make out Dad standing beside the couch in his robe.

"What are you doing out here?" he asked. And before I could answer, he said, "You're waiting for Lester, aren't you?"

I could feel my eyes closing again.

"And you turned off the alarm for him, didn't you?"

I opened my eyes. "I . . . I promised."

Dad didn't say any more. He sat down on a chair across the room, his hands on his knees. I was afraid that if I got up and started for bed, he'd make me sit back down again, so I stayed where I was, wondering when the scolding would begin and what my punishment would be. I didn't know what time it was or how long I had been asleep, but I was certainly awake now.

It was just a few minutes later, though, that I heard our car pull up outside. A car door closed, probably as quietly as a car door could. It certainly didn't slam.

There were soft footsteps on the front steps, a key turned in the lock, and then the door was opening, but only a little way. I knew Lester had noticed the light on in the hall and knew someone was up.

"Come on in, Les," said Dad.

The front door opened wider, and Lester stepped into the hall. "D-Dad?" His eyes traveled over to me on the couch and asked the question I couldn't answer.

"This is the second time in the last month or so that I've been disappointed in the two of you," Dad said. "Lester, you should know better than to ask your sister to lie for you."

"Dad, you just don't understand!" Lester said. "This is a special night, and Lisa's a really nice girl. She works at a *book*store, Dad! I couldn't just give her a box of candy without talking to her a little while."

"Les, you had a lot of options. You could have given

it to her last weekend. You could have given it to her today at school. I'm not so old that I can't understand how a girl can be special and a night can be special, but this wasn't that night. It's a school night, and you've got a big exam tomorrow."

"Dad, I'm ready for it! I—"

"Do you have any idea how it makes me worry when you come home an hour late? And then . . . to get Alice involved . . ."

"Dad, I'm sorry," Les began.

But all Dad said was, "There are going to be some changes around here. I don't know yet what they are, but there will be changes. Go to bed."

Lester shot me an angry look. "What the heck were you doing out here on the couch with a blanket around you?" he growled as he went down the hall to the bathroom.

I went back to bed and crawled under the covers. Why hadn't he explained to Dad about Lisa Shane and how much she needed a friend? I *knew* Dad would understand. It's Lester *I* don't understand. He and I were definitely not any friendlier toward each other than we were before.

I'll bet if Lester had a choice, he would even choose a new pair of sneakers before he'd choose me.

※ ※   13   ※ ※

Saving Lisa

Dad didn't say any more to us the next morning about changes. Lester and I were careful to put our dishes in the sink after breakfast and pick up our shoes in the living room so we wouldn't make him any angrier than he was, but Lester wouldn't even look at me, like I was dog doo or something. As though he wouldn't have got caught if I hadn't wrapped up in a blanket and waited for him on the couch.

After school I went to Donald's house, as I always do on Tuesdays. There was something about the way Mrs. Sheavers sat down with us for our snack that told me she wanted to talk. There were three glasses of Hi-C orange drink and three saucers of Oreo cookies, not two.

"So!" said Mrs. Sheavers. "How was Valentine's Day at your house, Alice?"

I wondered if she knew about Lester coming home late. "It was okay," I said.

"Did your dad go out for the evening and celebrate?"

"No . . . ," I said.

"No? Doesn't believe in St. Valentine's Day, huh?"

"Well, he brought home some chocolates," I said. "A customer gave them to him."

"Aha! Sounds like he has a girlfriend," said Mrs. Sheavers.

"I don't think so," I said.

She smiled as though we had a secret. "Not even that woman who works with him? Janice something?"

Then I got scared. If Mrs. Sheavers knew for sure that Dad didn't have a girlfriend, maybe *she* would start giving him chocolates.

"I don't know," I said. "Maybe."

And suddenly Donald said, "Do you know how elephants get cool?" Donald's like that. He'll completely change the subject. His mouth was full of Oreos, but he just spit the question out.

"They suck up water in their trunks and blow it over their backs," I said. Rosalind tells me this kind of stuff.

"But how do they cool themselves if they're not near a river?" asked Donald.

"Fan themselves with their ears?" I said.

"And what else?" asked Donald.

"I don't know."

"They blow snot out of their trunks and cover their bodies with that," said Donald.

"Donald!" said his mother. She put down the cookie she was eating.

"It's true," said Donald. "If you were riding on an elephant and it got hot and there wasn't any water, it would turn its trunk around and you would be covered with snot."

"Stop it," said his mother.

"Let's go look up elephants," I said quickly, afraid she was going to ask me more questions about Dad.

Donald and I got out his science encyclopedias and looked up elephants. I would have looked up anything—even snakes or centipedes—just to get away from Mrs. Sheavers.

At dinner that night I asked Dad who had given him the chocolates.

"A woman customer," he said, passing the lasagna to me.

"Same woman you took to a play a couple of weeks ago?" asked Lester.

"Yes. Sharon Jeffers. Nice lady. Lost her husband about a year ago."

I don't know why, when a woman's husband dies, people say she "lost her husband," like he'd wandered away from her at the mall or something.

I remembered what Mrs. Sheavers had said. "Is

Sharon Jeffers your girlfriend, Dad?" I asked.

"Just a friend," said Dad.

I wondered when Dad and Lester were going to get *real* girlfriends, not just girls who were friends.

I checked with the Secret Six the next day to see how much money we'd saved. We only had twelve dollars and eleven pennies. I began to worry that Lisa Shane would never have enough money to get away from her cruel parents. What if Lester *did* get a girlfriend—not just someone he felt sorry for? What if he forgot all about Lisa and her problems?

But when I came home from school, Lester was on the phone with Lisa as usual, and I heard him say, "It looks like someone beat you with a baseball bat."

I slowly hung up my jacket, listening.

"Don't give me that!" said Lester. ". . . They were too! There were even bruises on your knees!"

"Because I'm *concerned* about you, that's why," Lester was saying. Then he saw me listening. He picked up the phone and went around the corner toward the bathroom.

I knew I couldn't wait any longer. The next day at school the Secret Six met back by the fence at recess. I told them about the bruises on Lisa Shane's legs and how Lester said it looked like someone had beaten her with a baseball bat.

"Somebody should *do* something about that!" said Jody. "Her dad sounds mean enough to kill her."

"That's why we have to help her get to China!" I said. "Lester's worried too. I don't think we should wait until we save up twenty dollars. I think we should send what we have right now."

"Why don't we each bring something to school tomorrow to go in a box, and you can mail it to her along with our money?" said Megan.

"What should we bring?" asked Dawn.

"Food," said Rosalind.

"Medicine for her bruises. Salve or something," said Sara.

"Clothes?" Dawn asked.

"I don't know her size or anything. Maybe something she could wear in China," I told them.

When I was at the Sheaverses' after school that day, I asked Donald's mother if she had ever been to China. I wondered if she could tell me what they wore.

"No, but I know how to eat with chopsticks," she said. She opened a kitchen drawer and took out several pairs of chopsticks. WONG'S RESTAURANT, was printed on the sides.

Mrs. Sheavers put some bite-size shredded wheat in a bowl and showed me how to hold the chopsticks to pick up pieces of cereal. Donald pretended he was a robot with his sticks. One piece . . . two pieces . . .

three pieces . . . Up from the bowl and into his mouth.

"Uh-oh," said Donald. "Something's wrong with my automatic arm!" His hand picked up the next piece and put it in his ear.

"Stop that!" said his mother, and took his chopsticks away. "You can keep yours, Alice," she said.

When I went home later, I washed the chopsticks and wrapped them in tissue paper. I decided I would put them in the box for Lisa Shane.

On Friday all sorts of little packages appeared at school, and I stuffed them in my book bag. It was so full, I could hardly close the zipper. There were lumps and bumps all over.

"It looks like a pregnant cat," said Rosalind.

"Is that what a cat looks like that's going to have kittens?" I asked.

"I think so," she told me.

"I am never, ever going to have babies!" I declared. "I don't want bumps sticking out all over me."

"Me either," said Rosalind.

When I got home from school, I took my book bag to my room. I waited until I heard Lester playing CDs in the basement. Then I spread everything out on my bed to see what the Secret Six had collected.

Twelve dollars and eleven pennies; a jar of salve; a gray Ocean City sweatshirt, size large; a folding paper fan made in Taiwan; a bar of soap; and a box of Pop-Tarts.

I added my pair of chopsticks and the thong beach sandals from Aunt Sally. Then I looked in all my dresser drawers. I searched the kitchen cupboards. I found a tube of toothpaste, a pair of white socks—one size fits all—a little box of raisins, a comb, and a bag of rice.

I got a small cardboard box from our storage closet and put all our stuff in it. Then I took a sheet of tablet paper and wrote a letter:

> Dear Lisa,
>
> We hope this will help you buy an airplane ticket and go where your father will never find you. Don't tell your mother, either, or she'll probably tell him where you are. Here is some salve for your bruises and some other things you can use in China.
>
> Sincerely yours,
> The Secret Six

I taped the box shut. Then I found Lisa's number on the back of our phone book, where Lester had written it. I looked up *Shane* in the phone book and went down the column until I found the address that went with that number.

I didn't know how much it would cost to mail the box, though, so I pried the bottom off my piggy bank and took out all the money. I stuffed it in my jeans, and the next morning, when Dad was at work and Lester was still sleeping, I slipped out the door and walked five blocks to the post office.

It took only a few dollars from my piggy bank money to mail it. I know I'm supposed to be saving that for college or something unless it's really, really important. But if saving a girl from being beaten with a baseball bat isn't important, I don't know what would be.

I felt good all weekend. I wanted so much to tell Lester what a wonderful thing the Secret Six had done for his friend, but we wanted it to be surprise. I guess one way you know you are growing up is if you can keep a secret.

On Monday all the girls wanted to know if I had mailed the package yet, and I told them I had.

"I'll bet we'll go to heaven for this," said Dawn.

I looked at her. "Are we going to die?" I asked.

"I mean, when we *do* die, we'll go to heaven. God will write it down in his book," Dawn told us. "He puts those kinds of things down on one side of the page and the bad things on the other."

It sounded sort of like Santa Claus to me.

"What kind of bad things do you suppose He'll write down?" asked Sara.

"If you swear or cheat," said Megan.

"If you lie or steal," said Dawn. "Then you definitely won't go to heaven."

"Even if you lie only once?" I asked. I don't know a lot about heaven.

"If you ask God to forgive you, you're okay," said Dawn.

"What if He forgives you and you do it all over again?" Jody wanted to know.

"Then you have to get forgiven again," said Megan. Megan and Dawn know the most about God.

"You mean you can just keep cheating and stealing and getting forgiven and doing it all over again?" asked Rosalind.

"I think there's only a certain number of times; I'm not sure," said Dawn.

I decided I had a lot of learning to do before I could grow up to be kind and good, but at least I was getting smarter. Number one: I'd learned to keep a secret about the Secret Six; two: I was helping to save Lisa Shane's life; three: I was learning about God and heaven.

I wondered how long it would take for the package to get to Lisa's. I knew it probably had to go from one post office to another, and from there to Lisa's house. Maybe tomorrow, I thought. Or maybe the day after. But right this minute I'll bet God was writing in his book, *Alice Kathleen McKinley was kind to Lisa Shane.*

14

Liar! Liar!

As I walked home from school that afternoon I still felt good about myself. Saving Lisa Shane was probably the best thing I had ever done in my whole life.

What was the worst thing? I remember hiding my plate of Brussels sprouts under the sink at Aunt Sally's once and being scolded for that. And I scratched Lester once. More than once. I guess all that would be in God's book too.

Donald had walked home with some boys this time, and I was glad it was a Monday and I didn't have to go to his house. But when I walked up the front steps, I didn't even have time to open the door. Lester opened it for me.

"Al, you idiot!" he yelled. He grabbed my arm and pulled me inside.

"What?" I said, staring up at him.

"What have you been going around telling people?"

"*What?*" I said again.

"About *Lisa!*" he yelled. "She got called into the counselor's office because someone called the school and said that her father had beaten her with a baseball bat and she had bruises all over her legs."

Who could have called? "*I* didn't call the school!" I said. "I don't even know the number!"

"Well, who *did* you tell?" He wouldn't stop yelling. "Lisa was mortified! The counselor said that a little girl's mother had called and said that you'd told her daughter that Lisa had bruises all over her legs and that her father did it."

"I *heard* you say she had bruises!" I said hotly. "You said it looked like someone beat her with a baseball bat!"

"Al, she got those bruises in soccer practice! *Will you please stay out of my business?* Why did you say it was her father?"

"You told me yourself! You said her parents hated her and her father beat her every day and she could only eat scraps off the table and cried herself to sleep at night!"

Lester stared at me as though I had an eye in the middle of my forehead. "You *believed* that? Al, I was *joking!* Of course her father doesn't beat her!"

Now *I* was yelling. I swung my book bag at him and hit him on the knees. "You *lied* to me!" I cried. I didn't care if God was watching or not. I'll bet He was too busy writing down all the lies Lester had told. "You said she was adopted and her parents hated her and . . ."

I remembered all the money and stuff we had sent her and how I'd walked five blocks to the post office. I just kept swinging at Lester with my book bag, and my eyes were so teary, I couldn't even tell if I was hitting him or not. "I felt *sorry* for her, and all my friends felt sorry too, and all the time you were lying!" I cried. "Liar, liar, liar!"

Lester grabbed my book bag and threw it down the hall. He pushed me over to the couch and made me sit down. "Tell me exactly what you told everybody. Lisa's really mad at me."

"We just wanted to help her, Lester!" I said.

"Who's 'we'?"

"The Secret Six."

"*Who?*"

"Rosalind and Sara and Megan and Dawn and Jody and me."

"Man, oh, man," said Lester, and rested his head in his hands. "So you told them all that stuff. . . ."

"And we sent her some money too!" I said angrily.

Lester's head jerked up. "You sent her *money?*"

"Twelve dollars and eleven cents. You said she hardly got anything to eat and—"

"Her father's a *banker*! Her mom's a professor!"

I started to cry all over again. "It's your fault for lying, and God's going to write *you* down in his book!" I wept.

I heard Lester let out his breath. "Okay, start from the beginning," he said. "When did you send her the money?"

"Saturday," I sniffled. "In a box."

"A box? You sent money in a box?"

"With the other stuff," I said.

Lester's face looked like it was made out of rubber. The eyebrows kept rising higher and higher. "What other stuff?"

I tried to remember. "Well, there was a bar of soap and some socks and a sweatshirt and toothpaste . . ."

Now Lester's eyes looked like marbles. Big marbles.

I went on: ". . . and some chopsticks and a fan and beach sandals and a box of Pop-Tarts and a bag of rice."

"A bag of *rice*?"

"To eat in China."

"*China*?" Lester yelped.

"You said that's where she was going, Lester! To work in a rice paddy!"

Lester couldn't speak for a moment or two. Finally he asked, "How did you get her address?"

"You wrote her number on the back of the phone book. I matched it with an address under the name *Shane*."

"Al, do you have any idea of the trouble you've caused? If the counselor didn't already know Lisa and her family, she might have called the police! Lisa had to ask the whole soccer team to go down to the office and explain that she got those bruises in a pileup when they had their first practice last week! How could you be so dumb to believe all that stuff?"

"How could you tell me so much that isn't true?" I yelled back, and tried to hit him again, but he caught my hand.

"Whether you believed it or not, you had no right to go around telling everyone things that aren't any of your business!" he said.

"If a girl's getting beaten up by her father, it's everybody's business!" I told him.

"Can't you tell when I'm joking?"

"I'll never believe another thing you tell me, Lester! Never, ever, ever!" I bawled, tears running down my cheeks. "If you say you're failing high school, I'll just say, 'Yeah, right!' If you say your bike got stolen, I'll say, 'Ha! I'll bet!' If you tell me you're dying, Lester, I'll just laugh and say, 'Ha! Big joke.' I won't listen to you ever again."

We both sat glaring at each other.

"So whose mother called the school?" I asked finally. I didn't even want to *talk* to Lester ever again, but I had to find this out.

"I don't know," Lester growled. He hardly even opened his mouth as he spoke. "Jody somebody. Her mother's a nurse."

Boy! I thought. *Wait till I see Jody!* We promised never to tell! Jody wasn't my friend anymore and Lester was mad at me and Lisa was mad at Lester and the Secret Six would be *really* mad at me when I told them we had sent our money to a banker's daughter who wasn't going to work in a rice paddy after all.

I jumped up suddenly and stormed to my room. "I hate you!" I yelled. I banged my door and lay down on my bed and cried. God was probably so busy writing down all the bad things I'd said to Lester that He couldn't even take care of the starving children in India.

How could Lester lie to me and call it a joke? How could I have believed him? How could Jody break her promise? What would Lisa think of me when she opened the box? She was already mad at Lester because of me. When she opened our package and found a box of Pop-Tarts and some socks and . . . And then I remembered the letter. *We hope this will help you buy an airplane ticket and go where your father will never find you,* I'd written. *Here is some salve for your bruises . . .* I'd forgotten to tell Lester about the ointment.

Lester and I hardly spoke to each other at dinner. I just stared down at my plate, and Lester silently stuffed food into his mouth.

Finally Dad said, "Have you two taken a vow of silence, or are we going to have a little conversation tonight?"

Lester just grunted. "Go ahead and talk if you want, but Al's said enough for a while. Whatever you tell her, Dad, it will be all over the neighborhood in five minutes."

Dad looked at me and then at Lester. "Have I missed something?"

"Yes," said Lester. "Be grateful."

"It's all because he's a liar!" I said bitterly. "He tells me things and then gets mad because I believe him."

Dad sighed. "Okay," he said. "I won't ask. I've had a hard day too." We all ate for a while without talking.

The phone rang and Lester leaped up to answer, but it wasn't Lisa. It was a man wanting to clean our gutters. Lester came back to the kitchen and scooped up some ice cream for himself, but he didn't offer to dish up any for me.

Dad was still eating his meat loaf. He took another

bite and said, "I was going to fix rice for dinner, but I couldn't find any. I was sure I'd bought some the last time I was at the store. Do either of you know where it went?"

"Ask Al," said Lester. "She sent it to a banker's daughter."

15

Changes

On Wednesday when I got home from school, I went in my bedroom and found the box I had mailed to Lisa. She must have given it to Lester at school. He left a note on top of the box: *You ever do something like this again, I'll wring your neck.*

I felt a tear slip out of my eye and slide down one cheek. *This is what happens when you try to help someone!* I thought angrily. No wonder there's so much trouble in the world!

What I was really crying about, though, was knowing that I had to tell the Secret Six. I had to say that Lisa Shane was the daughter of a banker and her parents loved her very much and she wasn't going to China after all.

I figured it would be easier telling them one at a time.

Both Megan and Rosalind live on my street. So I carried the box down to Megan's house first and said I had to talk to her in private.

"What do you want to tell her?" asked Marlene, her little sister, who opened the door.

"None of your business," I said, and made a terrible face at her. Sometimes when you pass a baby in a stroller, you can make him cry if you put on a terrible face. I only do that when I'm feeling mean and grumpy, but Marlene was too old to be scared.

Megan saw me standing at the door, though, and told me to come on up to her room. She was looking at the box in my arms and closed the door behind us. I gulped out the story.

"Lisa didn't even have bruises?" Megan asked.

"Soccer practice," I said.

"She's not going to work in a rice paddy?"

"No."

"Well, I think it's all Lester's fault for telling you that," said Megan. She took back the sweatshirt and the money she had given. "I think I'll use this money to do something nice for someone else."

Megan will go to heaven for sure. *I* was thinking I could use mine to go to the movies! And then she said something even nicer. "Do you want me to call Jody and Dawn for you and tell them what happened?"

I nodded. "Except that I've got something to say to

Jody myself!" I said, thinking how it was Jody's mom who'd called the high school about Lisa's bruises.

Next I went up the street to Rosalind's. When she answered the door, she was holding a bag of potato chips. She held it out toward me. "Want some?"

I shook my head.

"Come on in," she said.

From somewhere in the house I could hear Rosalind's brother Billy playing his guitar. Her oldest brother goes to college, but he was there too, watching television. He was eating crackers and cheese on the sofa, and I just waved hi to him, because I've met him before.

"You want to make milk shakes?" Rosalind asked.

I shook my head. Then she saw the box. "What happened?" she asked.

"Let's go in your room," I told her, and we went down the hall. I had to tell the story all over again.

"So Lisa wasn't adopted?"

I shook my head. "I don't think so. Anyway, her parents love her."

"And they don't just give her scraps from the table?"

"No."

Rosalind took back the money and the box of Pop-Tarts she had given and opened the top. "Want one?" she asked.

"No, thanks," I said. "Megan says she's going to do something nice for someone with her money."

"Yeah!" said Rosalind. "Or the Secret Six could all go to Pizza Hut!"

"I guess we're not so secret anymore," I said. I looked around Rosalind's room. There are pictures and posters all over her walls, and they're all of animals. Monkeys and giraffes and hippos and otters. Elephants, too, of course. Rosalind is serious about working in a zoo.

Her stepmom came to the bedroom door just then. It's amazing—even though Rosalind wasn't born to her, they look so much alike! Their cheeks are round and their arms are round—everything about them is round. Rosalind's stepmom smiles more than Rosalind does, though.

"Hello, Alice. Would you like to stay for dinner?" she asked.

I would have loved to stay for dinner. I would have loved to stay all night, just so I wouldn't have to look at Lester being angry at me all the time. But I couldn't.

"Lester and I have to cook dinner tonight. Maybe some other time," I said.

"Sure. Just tell me what you like best, and I'll make it," she said, smiling.

I would have to write that down on my list of what a good mother would do: cook anything you wanted.

• • •

I kept remembering that Dad had told us there were going to be changes. I wondered if he had forgotten, because he hadn't said anything more. Maybe he figured that Lester and I could get along better and keep each other alive after all.

But Lester and I hardly spoke as we made dinner. I think Lisa was still mad at him and he was mad at me. We served canned chop suey over canned chow mein noodles, with canned peas for a vegetable. And suddenly, right in the middle of dinner, Dad put down his fork and said, "I thought you should know that I've hired a woman named Mrs. Nolinstock to be here three afternoons a week and all day on Saturdays. She will look after things and cook and clean for us too. And when Mrs. Nolinstock is here, she's completely in charge. I want that understood."

Lester and I stared at him. He was hiring someone to take *care* of us? Lester too?

"Dad!" said Lester. "Three afternoons a week plus Saturdays? It will cost you a fortune, and besides, Al and I can cook!"

"Well, it might be nice to have some meals occasionally that don't come out of a can. It might be nice to have a vegetable once in a while besides peas," said Dad.

"But we can take care of ourselves!" I told him.

"Apparently not," said Dad. "When I get a call that

you were rescued out of a snowbank, and Lester doesn't come home when he's supposed to, and lately, it seems, you two aren't even talking to each other, I think maybe we ought to make other arrangements. As I said, when Mrs. Nolinstock is here, I expect you to do as she says."

I just went on staring at Dad. He never looked more serious in his life. Lester got up and left the kitchen.

The next day at school I walked up to Jody and said, "How could you do that? How could you tell your mother about Lisa Shane when we promised we wouldn't tell *anyone*?"

Jody was ready for me: "Because when you think someone's getting beaten by her father, it's not the kind of secret anyone should keep," she said.

"Then you shouldn't have promised!" I told her.

"I didn't think about it at the time. It was only that night, when I wondered if right that minute her dad was beating her with a baseball bat, that I figured I ought to tell my mom about it. And that's when she said that you should never keep that kind of secret."

"Well, you got me and Lester and Lisa in a lot of trouble," I said.

"Tough," said Jody. "Lester shouldn't have lied in the first place. Megan told me all about it."

"Well, now Lester's mad at me. And Lisa sent the

box back." I pointed to my back pack. "I don't know what you gave her, but you can have it back."

Mr. Dooley asked us to be quiet then while he started our math lesson. I would have been quiet anyway. I didn't want to talk to Jody anymore, and she didn't want to talk to me.

16

Nolinstock

It was a miserable afternoon. I felt even more miserable the next day when I remembered that Mrs. Nolinstock would be at my house after school, waiting to take care of me. I told Donald, and he said he'd like to see what a Nolinstock looked like. We went up the front steps. The door was locked. I had to ring the bell.

For a minute we didn't think anyone would answer. Then the door opened, and there stood a tall, thin woman with gray-brown hair pulled back from her forehead and tied with a rubber band in back. She was wrinkled around the eyes, but her face was bright pink and her mouth was as straight across as a ruler. She was wearing a brown sweater and a brown skirt and low-heeled brown shoes that were so wide, they looked like duck feet. I'll bet if she had smiled, which she didn't, even her teeth would be brown.

"Are you Mrs. Nolinstock?" I asked, hoping she wasn't.

"Yes," she said. "Are you Alice?"

I nodded. "And this is Donald," I said. "He lives next door."

"Then Donald should go next door," said Mrs. Nolinstock, giving him a quick nod. "All children should go directly home after school so their mothers know where they are."

She opened the door wider for me and closed the door on Donald.

I stared at her. "That was rude!" I said.

"That was *necessary*," she answered. "I like to make my rules plain from the very first day. We will all get along better if we know what they are. And how was your day at school, Alice?"

"Crummy," I said, and I wasn't smiling.

Something was cooking in the kitchen—chicken, I guess—and it probably smelled good, but right then everything about Mrs. Nolinstock seemed awful. When she went back out to the kitchen, I even saw her lift Oatmeal out of the way with her foot.

I sat down in the living room beside the coffee table and opened my school notebook. I tried to see how many words I could make out of *Nolinstock* by mixing the letters up: *tin, sin, lost, ink, oink, stink, snoot, snot. . . .*

Mrs. Nolinstock went on working out in the kitchen, but after a while she came to the doorway and looked in on me. "Do you have any homework to do this afternoon, Alice?" she asked.

"A little," I said, trying not to look at the way her thin lips hardly opened when she talked.

"And have you finished it all?" she asked.

"Not quite," I said. "Almost."

"*Almost* and *not quite* won't do," she said. "You wouldn't want a pilot who *almost* got the plane to fly but *not quite,* would you?"

How did we get talking about airplanes all of a sudden? I wondered. How did we get talking about pilots? How did my dad find this woman, anyway?

"I can easily do it over the weekend," I told her.

"Never put off until tomorrow what you can do today," she said.

After she went back in the kitchen, I took a piece of notebook paper and in big black letters I printed: *DANGER: NOLINSTOCK INSIDE!* I taped it to the outside of the front door. Lester's school gets out first, so he's usually home before me, but this time, I figured, he'd be hiding out.

After a while I heard his footsteps, then a key in the lock, and finally the front door opened a crack. Lester peeked inside. I put one finger to my lips.

"Where is she?" he whispered.

I pointed to the kitchen. The basement door was just this side of the kitchen, and I knew he wanted to sneak down there before she saw him, but it was too late.

"Are you Lester?" she asked, suddenly appearing in the doorway, and Lester stopped in his tracks. "I'm Mrs. Nolinstock. Glad to meet you. How's your homework?"

Lester didn't miss a beat. "Fine," he said. "How's yours?"

Mrs. Nolinstock was not amused. She just stared back at Lester with her lips in their fine straight line and said, "Dinner's at six thirty," and went back out to the kitchen.

I followed Lester down to the basement. I tried to imagine coming home three days a week to find Mrs. Nolinstock there. I tried to imagine waking up on Saturday mornings after Dad went to work and knowing that *she* was in our kitchen.

"Isn't she awful?" I said. "She was so rude to Donald."

"Has she smiled even once since you got home?" Lester asked.

I shook my head. "How long is she going to be working here, Lester? Till we're grown? Till we're married?"

"Dad can't afford this!" said Lester. "We've got to think of a way to get rid of her."

I wasn't sure what Lester had in mind, because I

remembered how he'd got rid of my Barbie doll by sticking her head in a vise. "How?" I asked.

"We just have to make her not want to work here anymore," he told me.

"Lester, I think we are going to get ourselves in big, big trouble if we make her quit," I said.

"And what do you think will happen if Mrs. Nolinstock stays?" asked Lester.

I thought about it a moment. "Big, *big* trouble," I said.

The problem was that the dinner Mrs. Nolinstock made for us was pretty good. There was roast chicken and real mashed potatoes and gravy, not the kind you mix. There were cooked beets and green beans with onions.

Dad ate second helpings of everything. So did Lester. Score: Mrs. Nolinstock, one; Lester and me, zero.

The next time she came, her cooking was even better: pot roast with carrots and potatoes and a big green salad. She made a chocolate pie for dessert. How could she cook so good and sound so sour? I wondered.

She never said, *You look as though you could use a cookie* or *Beautiful day, isn't it?* She'd just give me a nod and say something like, "Be sure to hang up your jacket" or—if I got down the peanut butter and crackers— "You don't want to ruin your appetite."

When Lester came home, she didn't seem able to

walk into a room without saying, "Feet off the coffee table" or "Do I see a soda can on the arm of the couch?" Once, when Mickey called, he took the phone into the closet to talk. After he had been in there for thirty minutes, Mrs. Nolinstock knocked on the door and told him his time was up, that someone might be trying to reach us.

"Where did you find Mrs. Nolinstock, Dad? Some company called Rent-a-Nazi?" he asked one night after she'd gone home. "Is she a retired warden from a state prison?"

"A customer gave me her name," Dad told us. "He said she was good at running a household with an iron hand. And I have to say that I enjoy finding clean clothes in my drawers, and a nutritious meal on the table, and having the peace of mind of knowing that the house won't burn down while I'm at work."

"But she's got to be expensive, Dad! She'll bankrupt us. There goes my college tuition."

"Well, it's nice to know you're concerned, Les," Dad said. "Every time I've tried to talk to you about college, you say you don't know."

Lester sighed. "Well, I've made up my mind to go to Montgomery College, then transfer to a university after I decide on a major."

"Good decision!" said Dad. "So you *have* been doing some thinking."

I liked the thought that Lester would be going to college around here, even if he *was* mad at me a lot. Besides Dad and Oatmeal, he's the only family I've got.

Dad helped himself to another spoonful of creamed corn. "I take it you two don't care much for Mrs. Nolinstock?"

Lester and I both made gagging noises.

"If you like living with an army general, she's great," said Lester. "If you like being ordered to wipe your feet, pick up your towel, and do your homework, she's tremendous. If you like being in the same house with a commander in chief who times you when you make a phone call, she's the best."

"I'm glad you appreciate her finer qualities," Dad said, and took another pork chop.

While Lester and I were doing the dishes later, he said, "If she just came to do the cooking and left, I could stand it."

"Yeah, her pies are great, but I can't think of anything to make her leave," I said. Dad and I could make only three kinds of pies. Mrs. Nolinstock made a different pie every time she came over.

If only I could think of a way to get rid of Mrs. Nolinstock, Lester wouldn't be mad at me anymore and Dad would save a lot of money. Dawn told me she prays when she wants God to help her with something, but I didn't think God would want to help me with this.

17

Good News, Bad News, Worse News

When April came, we turned over a new page on the school calendar. Then we tried to play tricks on each other, just so we could say "April fool!" But Mr. Dooley wasn't there to play tricks with us. There was a substitute teacher named Miss Beck. She told us she got a phone call that morning saying Mr. Dooley wouldn't be in. She didn't know why.

"I'll bet Mrs. Dooley had her baby," said Sara.

"The baby's not due till April twelfth," said Rosalind.

"Sometimes they come early," said Sara, and she should know because she's got a whole bunch of brothers and sisters.

When lunchtime came, though, and there still wasn't any news about Mr. Dooley's baby, I began to worry. Maybe something bad happened. Maybe the baby died.

Maybe it was alive but something was terribly wrong with it. Aunt Sally told me once about a baby who had been born with water on the brain and its head was too big for its body. Maybe the little cap I'd given Mr. Dooley's baby didn't fit. Maybe it would never fit.

"How long does it take to have a baby?" I asked Sara at recess that afternoon.

"Sometimes it takes all day," she said. Her mother had had her last baby at home, so she knew, she told us.

"Did you watch it come out?" asked Jody.

"No. It was the middle of the night," Sara said. "Besides, it's messy."

I wondered then if babies were born in the bathtub and if you could just rinse them off and wash the rest down the drain.

That afternoon we were having our geography lesson when Mr. Serio came in our room. He said he had some news for us, and his face was very serious. It was about Mr. Dooley's baby, he said. I think I stopped breathing.

But then the principal started to smile. "It's a boy," he said, "and the baby and his mother are doing just fine."

We all started to clap.

"What's the baby's name?" Megan asked.

"I don't know. I'll let Mr. Dooley tell you when he comes back next week," Mr. Serio said.

I didn't stop smiling the rest of the day.

. . .

I thought of a way I might be able to make Mrs. Nolinstock quit. When I got home that afternoon, Mrs. Nolinstock asked if I had any homework.

"No, ma'am," I said.

She paused. "Did you get it all done at school, then?" she asked.

"No, ma'am," I said.

She studied me for a moment. "Are you putting it off until later?" she asked.

"No, ma'am," I said.

She went back to the kitchen. I decided I wouldn't say anything else to her except "Yes, ma'am" and "No, ma'am" for as long as she worked at our house. That would drive her crazy, but at least she couldn't tell Dad I was rude! The house smelled good, though. It smelled like cinnamon.

When Lester came home, I told him just to say "Yes, ma'am" and "No, ma'am." He sat down on the couch with the sports section of the *Washington Post*. He put one foot on the coffee table. Mrs. Nolinstock came to the doorway.

"Feet off the table," she said.

"Yes, ma'am," said Lester, and put his foot on the floor.

"Homework?" she asked.

"Yes, ma'am," said Lester.

"You'll be getting right on it, then?"

"Yes, ma'am," said Lester, and went right on reading the newspaper. I laughed and Lester even smiled a little. I figured she would quit that very day.

But when Dad got home and Mrs. Nolinstock put on her jacket, she said, "See you Wednesday," and left. *Yes, ma'ams* and *no, ma'ams* didn't bother her at all.

That evening Lester said, "Dad, did you know that all the seniors at school have their own cars?"

"You've taken a poll?" said Dad.

"*Everyone* has a car when he's a senior," Lester said. "I think we should get one for me this summer so I can start driving to school next fall."

"We're three blocks from the high school, Lester. Surely your legs will carry you three blocks."

Lester jabbed at the chicken and dumplings Mrs. Nolinstock had made for us. "Maybe you didn't have a car when you were a senior, but it'll make me feel like a freak if I don't. Some of the juniors have one already! Lisa has a car. Even *Mickey* has a car! How am I supposed to ask a girl out when I don't have a car?"

"You can always use mine, Les."

"But I can't use it during the day! I can't drive a girl home from school. I can't take the guys to the deli."

"Les, until you have a real reason to own a car, you're going to have to share mine," said Dad. "And we certainly are not going to buy you a car until you have a part-time job and can earn the insurance money yourself."

"You said I couldn't have a job until summer!"

"That's right. I want you to concentrate on your grades."

"So how can I get the money to pay for insurance? The last two years of high school are the most important, Dad! Lisa will never go out with me if I don't have a car. None of the girls will want to go out with me. I'm a dork, a freak, a nerd, a nobody!"

The phone rang just then, and I hoped it was Lisa telling him she liked him even without a car. *Mickey,* even. But it wasn't. Lester answered, and then he came back in the kitchen.

"Dad, it's Aunt Sally," he said. "And she's crying."

We all stopped eating. *Uncle Milt!* I thought. Something must have happened to my uncle. Dad jumped up and went to the phone.

"I hope nothing's happened to Carol," said Lester. He and our cousin Carol have always been great buddies.

I swallowed what was in my mouth, but I didn't take any more bites. I don't like to think about people dying. Since I was born, my mom has died, Uncle Charlie's died, and so has Lester's dog. I felt I just couldn't stand for it to happen to someone else.

"Sal, I can certainly understand how upsetting this is," we heard Dad say.

"Maybe *she's* sick," Lester said to me in a low voice.

It seemed a long time before Dad came back to the table.

"What is it?" asked Lester.

"What's happened?" I said.

Dad sighed and shook his head. "Carol's eloped," he said. "With a sailor." He sat back down.

Eloped? Wasn't that when a woman climbs out of her window and runs off with her boyfriend to get married?

"She climbed down a ladder?" I asked, still trying to figure it out.

"No, Al. She was a student at Northwestern near Chicago, remember? Sal just found out that Carol left school and went off one weekend and got married."

"Oh," I said. Then, "What's so awful about that?"

Dad looked at me in surprise. "Number one, she's only nineteen, and that's pretty young to be settling down with someone for life. Number two, Sal and Milt don't even know this sailor. Number three, Carol's their only child, and Sal had always imagined a big wedding with all the relatives there. I know it hurts that Carol didn't even tell them."

"Hey! When a person gets married, I think she should have it any way she wants. And how do you know the sailor's not a really nice guy?" said Lester.

"Well, maybe if you were a parent, you'd feel differently," said Dad.

"So where are they now?" asked Lester.

"On a honeymoon in Mexico. Carol just called."

"What does Aunt Sally want *you* to do? Go after them?" I asked.

"No. She just wanted to talk. She had such high hopes for that girl. Carol's been a free spirit since the day she was born, though."

"And the most interesting person in that family," said Lester.

"Les . . . ," Dad said, and then he looked at me, too. "Al . . . I don't think I could take any more shocks to my nervous system. Promise me one thing: If either of you ever considers eloping, getting a tattoo, buying a motorcycle, or going bungee jumping, just give me a little warning, huh? Break it to me gently?"

"Sure, Dad," said Lester.

"I promise," I said.

I thought about Aunt Sally and Uncle Milt being sad. I thought about Aunt Sally wanting to plan a wedding for Carol, and now there wasn't any wedding at all. Somehow Lester's problem about not having a car didn't seem so important after that.

18

April in Maryland

Mr. Dooley came back to school after spring vacation. He looked tired and happy. The skin under his eyes was sort of blue, but all he did was smile.

We crowded around his desk to see pictures of the baby.

"His name is Elijah David Dooley," he told us. "He weighs seven pounds, ten ounces, and he has blue eyes and brown hair. All he does is eat and sleep and wet and poop and cry, and he's absolutely wonderful."

We passed the pictures around. There was a photo of Elijah David Dooley sleeping with his thumb in his mouth. Elijah David crying with his toothless mouth wide open. Elijah in his mother's arms. Elijah having his first bath in the sink. And there was a picture of Elijah David Dooley wrapped in a blanket and wearing the little blue knit cap that said HAPPY BIRTHDAY, BEETHOVEN on the front in white letters.

I smiled at Mr. Dooley and he smiled back. When the last bell rang at the end of the day, Mr. Dooley said he'd made an extra copy of the picture of Elijah in his new cap, and it was for me.

Everything seemed fresh and new when I walked home from school that afternoon. The trees had more leaves, flowers were beginning to bloom, and the air smelled warm and clean. I would be ten years old in May, and I thought maybe this would be a new start for me. Ten seemed very grown up.

But I didn't feel grown up that night when I went to bed. Dad came in my room as usual to read to me—I still like him to read aloud—but I was thinking about the picture of Mrs. Dooley holding her baby.

Dad read another chapter of *The Incredible Journey*, then asked if I wanted to read a chapter to him. I shook my head and just lay there on my side, holding on to my pillow.

"When I was little—when I was just born, I mean— did Mother hold me and rock me too?" I asked.

I couldn't see Dad's face because he was sitting behind me on the edge of the bed, but I could hear the surprise in his voice. "Of course!" he said. "She hardly ever wanted to let you go. I almost had to beg for a chance to hold you myself."

I kept staring at the wall. "Did she feed me from her breast?"

"Sure. Sometimes when she needed to sleep, I gave you a bottle. But most of the time she nursed you; you got your milk from her."

"And did she give me a bath in the sink?"

"In a basin, I think. Don't you remember those pictures in your baby book, Alice?"

He got up and went into his bedroom, then came back with my baby book in its white silk cover. BABY DEAR, it said in pink letters. I guess I remembered the pictures. Dad held the book while I turned the pages. There I was, asleep in my crib, my knees drawn up to my chest, my behind in the air. Another picture of Mother in a swing, holding me on her lap. Mother feeding me strained spinach. Mother giving me a bath.

"It's not fair," I said finally.

"I know it's not fair," said Dad quietly. "Nobody should have to lose her mother when she's only five years old."

"I mean about remembering," I said. "It's not fair that I can't remember her. The way she held me and all the things we did."

"No, it's not," said Dad.

"And it's not fair that she had to die before she could see me start first grade and lose my teeth and get a cat," I said, and my chin wobbled.

"Not a bit fair," said Dad.

I turned around and snuggled up against Dad's leg. "What would happen to me if something happened to you?" I asked.

"Well, I'm going to try hard not to let something bad happen to any of us," said Dad. "But there's Aunt Sally and Uncle Milt and Uncle Howard and Uncle Harold. One of them would take you in, don't you worry."

"Lester too?"

"Sure."

"We wouldn't have to go to an orphanage?"

"Of course not."

"Lester wouldn't just . . . give me away for somebody else to raise, would he?"

"Heavens no."

I hugged his leg even harder. "Drive carefully, Daddy," I said.

"I will," he told me.

On Saturday, Dad was at work, Lester was out looking for a summer job, and Mrs. Nolinstock was in the kitchen making a turkey casserole and another pie. A butterscotch pie this time, my favorite. She had her cooking things spread all over the kitchen table, so I sat on a high stool eating my breakfast at the counter.

"Did you go to cooking school or what?" I asked. I had stopped saying just "Yes, ma'am" and "No, ma'am," not because I liked her any better, but because it got boring.

Mrs. Nolinstock didn't answer. When she cooks, she whispers the recipe aloud to herself: "Three eggs, one and one-half cups milk . . . ," she said, and opened the refrigerator.

I guessed she was going to be as rude to me as I had been to her.

"Or did you just learn all this stuff yourself?" I went on.

". . . six tablespoons flour, one and one-third cups brown sugar . . . ," she continued. I didn't want her to make a mistake on our butterscotch pie, so I didn't ask any more questions.

When she had everything mixed, though, and started stirring, she said, "I taught myself."

I watched a while longer, her wooden spoon scraping the sides of the pan. "How do you know when it's done?"

"The pie filling gets thick," she said, and held up the spoon to show how the mixture was clinging to it.

My toast popped in the toaster and I buttered it. "Do you have any kids?" I asked.

"No, it's just me and Mr. Nolinstock and our work," she answered.

"No pets?"

"No time," she said.

"What kind of work does Mr. Nolinstock do?"

"He's a bookkeeper," she told me. Then she took the pan off the stove and held it out so I could see the thick golden pudding inside. "Now we cool it before we pour it in the pie shell," she said, and began washing the spoons and bowls and measuring cups.

"What do you do for fun?" I asked, studying the way her hair stuck straight out in back, caught by the rubber band.

She paused a moment and looked over at me as though she hadn't understood the question. "*This* is fun," she answered. "My work is fun."

I didn't think she had understood at all. "I mean, if you could be doing anything you wanted right now, what would it be?" I asked.

"Exactly what I'm doing right now," said Mrs. Nolinstock. "Making a meal that someone will enjoy."

Imagine that! Mrs. Nolinstock was having fun! I didn't know you could work and have fun both at the same time. She's sort of like my dad, I guess. He likes being manager of a music store so much that we moved all the way here from Chicago just for that.

Rosalind and Sara came over that afternoon. Rosalind had a new camera and wanted to take a whole roll of silly pictures. We made all the stupid faces we could think of. Sara and I pushed our noses up with one finger and pulled down the skin under our eyes with the others.

Click went the camera.

Rosalind and Sara hung coat hangers over their ears while I held the camera.

Click.

We stuck pieces of black licorice on some of our teeth so it looked like teeth were missing, and we took turns with the camera.

Click, click, click.

Then Sara put two large buttons over her eyes and scrunched up her face a little to hold them there while I took a picture.

Rosalind wedged a comb between her lips so that it stretched her mouth wide, and Sara took a picture of that.

Then I got two green vitamin pills and put them in my nostrils to look like I had a nose full of snot. Sara and Rosalind howled.

"That's disgusting." Rosalind laughed and started to take my picture, but one of the pills fell out. I put it back in and Rosalind lifted the camera again, but the pill fell out just like before. The next time I pushed it up farther still and tilted my head a little so the picture would show green stuff hanging out of my nostrils, and Sara covered her eyes because it looked so gross.

After the picture was taken, I got one of the vitamin pills out but not the other. When I tried to pry it out with my finger, I think I pushed it even farther back. It gave me a strange feeling in the back of my throat.

I looked at Rosalind and Sara in horror. Did this mean I was going to go the rest of my life with a vitamin pill stuck in my nostril? Would I graduate from high school with the pill still in my nose? When I was a bride, would I walk down the aisle with green stuff coming out of my nostrils?

"Whadab I gowig to do?" I gasped.

"Blow," said Rosalind.

I got a Kleenex and blew as hard as I could. Nothing happened. I could only breathe through one nostril.

"Don't try to get it out with your finger; you'll only push it farther in," said Sara. "My brother stuck a peanut up his nose once, and we had to take him to the emergency room."

I gave a little cry. The thought of having to tell Mrs. Nolinstock that I had something up my nose was almost worse than going to the hospital.

"Do you have any tweezers?" asked Rosalind. "Maybe we could operate."

"I dod wad you to operate!" I cried.

"But maybe I could reach it with tweezers," said Rosalind.

Now my nose began to run. Stuff started to come out. *Green* stuff!

"Euuuw!" said Rosalind. "Get the tweezers!"

I didn't know where we kept them. Lester had a pair, maybe. I went down in the basement to look through Lester's stuff, the girls behind me, and we opened the top drawer of his dresser.

Lester has a very messy drawer. Shoelaces, guitar picks, comb, socks, baseball cap, Band-Aids, Jockey shorts, a cassette . . .

"What are you doing?"

I think I jumped three inches off the floor as Lester came downstairs. "Get *out* of there!" he yelled at me. "Who said you could go through my dresser? Al, I want you to keep your nose out of my business and your hands out of my stuff!"

At the word *nose,* Rosalind pointed to mine. One side looked a little bit swollen, and the green stuff had dripped down to my upper lip. Lester stared at me.

"What's wrong with your nose?" he asked.

"She's got a vitamin pill in it," said Sara.

"How did *that* happen?" Les asked. "You *swallow* them, Al. You don't inhale them."

"We were looking for tweezers," I said, tears in my eyes.

"Well, you shouldn't be using tweezers, either," Lester said. "Didn't anyone ever tell you it's dangerous to fool around with your nostrils? You get an infection in your nose, it goes straight to the brain." He sounded as though he cared!

I started to cry, right there in front of Rosalind and Sara, and then my nose really dripped.

Lester reached into the bottom drawer·of his dresser and took out a flashlight. "Tip your head back," he said. I did. He shined the flashlight up my nose. "There's a vitamin pill up there, all right," he said.

What did he expect? A frog?

"Wait here," said Lester.

"Dod tell Bissus Dolidstock!" I begged, my nose even more clogged.

I sat down on the edge of Lester's bed. Rosalind and Sara just stood looking at me sorrowfully. I would be The Girl with the Green Snot who nobody ever wanted to play with. I would be The Girl with the Lump in Her Nose, and in high school I would be chosen The Grossest Girl Graduate and have to carry Kleenex with me wherever I went.

Lester came back from the kitchen with the pepper shaker. He sprinkled some in his hand and held it up to my nose. "Breathe in," he said.

I did the best I could with only one nostril open.

Ker-choo! I sneezed.

Nothing happened.

"Again," said Lester.

I stuck my nose in the pepper again, and Lester put one hand over my mouth.

Ker-CHOO! I went. The vitamin pill shot out of my nostril and hit the side of his wastebasket.

"*Thank* you, Lester!" I cried. "How did you know that would work?"

"Let's just say I have experience," he said. I was so relieved I wanted to hug him, but wasn't sure he'd let me. So I said, "I'll do something for you sometime."

"Don't even try," said Lester, and sent us back upstairs.

We went outside and sat on the steps.

"Think of all the things Elijah David has to learn," I said. "Not to run in front of cars, not to play with matches, not to stick vitamin pills up his nose. . . ."

"He'd never be dumb enough to do that," said Sara.

19

The No-Birthday Birthday

When I thought about all the things that had happened in fourth grade, I decided that nine years old
was the worst year of my life so far, except for the year
my mother died. No matter what I did, it always made
things worse between Lester and me.

Then he went and ruined my tenth birthday. Dad
had the flu first, and just after he got well, Lester got it
next, two days before my party.

I had already given out invitations to my friends. I
had folded sheets of paper into fourths and written a
name of a friend on each one in yellow and green and
copper. I had drawn stars and flowers, coated them
with glue, and sprinkled pink and green sparkles over
the glue, then tipped the paper so the extra stuff fell

off. The invitations were absolutely beautiful, but then I had to cancel the party.

"We'd better not, honey," Dad said. "We only have one bathroom, and Lester's in it. I don't think he'd appreciate girls running around out here while he was in there throwing up."

"Well, I don't appreciate him being sick," I said. I knew it sounded awful, but I said it anyway.

Dad raised one eyebrow. "It's not as though he planned it," he told me. "And remember, you may be next."

I hadn't even thought about that! Not on my tenth birthday! "God wouldn't do that, would He? Make me sick on my birthday?" I asked.

"God doesn't make people sick," said Dad. "Germs do. And people who live together share their germs."

That's when I got mad at Lester. When he came out of the bathroom in his pajamas, he sank down at the other end of the couch, and I scooted as far away from him as I could get.

"Keep your germs to yourself," I told him.

He just looked at me with saggy eyes. Then he got up, went in the bathroom, and threw up all over again.

When you hear someone else throw up, something happens to your throat. *I will not get sick,* I told myself. *I will not throw up. If I feel like throwing up, I will think about sucking ice cubes.*

"I'll tell you what, Al," said Dad. "Maybe we could take you and your friends to a movie on Sunday and go out for ice cream afterward. Is there a movie you'd like to see?"

I got the newspaper and we looked through the movie section together.

"*Night of the Assassin*," said Dad. "That's out."

"What's *assassin*?" I asked.

"A killer. A murderer," said Dad. "What else can you find?"

"*Secluded Weekend?*" I said, reading the ads. "*Lust and Lies?*"

"Keep looking," said Dad.

We couldn't find any good movies.

"Maybe we could go to a ball game," Dad suggested.

"Keep looking," I said.

Lester was still sick on Sunday, though, and Dad said he was really sorry, but he guessed there would be no birthday party for me this year. The following weekend he was going to be busy on Friday, Saturday, and Sunday too, so we couldn't have my party then. When Lester was better, though, he promised, the three of us would go out to dinner.

I folded my arms over my chest and let my lower lip stick out so far that Dad said he could hang a bucket on it. "All right," I said in a soft and whiny voice.

· · ·

At my school, kids bring cupcakes or cookies on their birthdays to share with the class. Dad told Mrs. Nolinstock that Sunday was my birthday, and on Saturday she baked me a four-layer cake. You can't very well take a four-layer cake to school, especially when there will be three pieces missing. So Dad drove me to school Monday morning, and we stopped at the Giant on the way and bought two dozen chocolate chunk cookies. Rosalind said that a big four-inch chocolate chunk cookie was almost better than a party. We had one extra, and she ate that one too.

I had a piece of birthday cake the day Mrs. Nolinstock made it. I had two pieces of birthday cake the next day, my real birthday. On Monday I had a chocolate chunk cookie at school and two more pieces of birthday cake for dinner. And then I got sick.

"Happy birthday," Lester said when I came out of the bathroom after throwing up the cake. "Sorry I didn't give you anything."

"You gave me something, all right, Lester," I said. "You gave me your germs."

"Enjoy!" said Lester, and went down in the basement to get ready for school the following day. He was feeling better, and I was sick.

But the next day I was better too.

"It wasn't the flu," said Dad. "It was the cake. Did

you ever thank Mrs. Nolinstock for making you a cake?"

"It made me sick!" I said.

"Only because you ate too much of it," said Dad.

So on Wednesday, when Mrs. Nolinstock came again, I went out in the kitchen where she was making rice pudding.

"Thank you for the cake," I said.

Mrs. Nolinstock went on stirring. "I'm glad you liked it," she said.

"It was delicious," I told her. "Except for the part I threw up."

If Mrs. Nolinstock was going to be around forever, I decided, then maybe she ought to know why we didn't like her and maybe she would change. Sometimes Lester didn't come home on the days she was there until it was almost time for her to leave. That's pretty bad, I think, when a person doesn't even want to walk into his very own house.

I decided to write Mrs. Nolinstock a letter. I wouldn't sign my name, but I would tell her why we didn't like her:

Dear Mrs. N,

You make good food, but the reason
we don't like you is you hardly ever

smile and you were rude to Donald.
You don't say nice things, either, to
Alice and her brother. They can take
care of themselves.

> Yours truly,
>
> A friend

P.S. You're also mean to her cat.

On Thursday, I left the letter in the vegetable bin in our refrigerator because we hardly ever look in there. I thought she would find it on Friday when she came back to cook. But Mrs. Nolinstock didn't find it. Dad did.

"Alice Kathleen McKinley!" he yelled that evening.

I went out in the kitchen. I thought maybe I'd forgotten to clean up after my snack. Dad was holding a piece of paper.

"Did you write this?" he asked.

"What is it?" I asked, though I recognized the yellow notebook paper from clear across the kitchen.

Dad handed the note to me. I sniffed it. "It smells like broccoli," I said.

"Did you *write* it?" asked Dad.

"I guess so," I said.

"Do you know what would have happened if Mrs. Nolinstock had found this?" he asked.

"She'd quit?" I asked hopefully.

"You would have really hurt her feelings," he said. "It was a rude thing to do."

"Well, she's been rude too, and I was just saying what I felt."

"You didn't even sign your name! Only cowards do that."

"If I sign my name, can we put it back with the broccoli?" I asked.

"No!" yelled Dad. He crumpled up the paper and threw it away.

"Well," I told Lester later, "I tried."

Sara invited me to her house on Saturday. She has a whole lot of brothers and sisters and a messy house with a chain-link fence around it.

First we played with some big wooden boxes in her backyard. Her dad got them from the company where he works. We stacked them on top of each other and made a fort. Then we put them side by side, and we all climbed in and pretended we were dead people. Sara said a prayer over us, and we rose from the dead and we were ghosts.

At two o'clock we were hungry, so we all went inside. Sara opened the refrigerator and called out what was in it.

"Cheese?" she said.

"Yeah!" said one of her brothers.

"Salami?" she said, taking out a package.

"I want some!" said a sister.

Sara kept taking out stuff—pickles and cold macaroni and lettuce and leftover sausage and corn and carrots—until there was enough to eat. We ate whatever we wanted. We didn't use forks. We ate cold macaroni with our fingers. It was delicious.

Sara's mother came in to get some iced tea. "Did you find everything you need?" she asked us.

"Yes," I said. "It was very good."

That's one of the differences between Rosalind's house and Sara's. At Sara's they stop doing other things sometimes to eat. At Rosalind's they stop eating sometimes to do other things.

Near the end of May, Dad took Lester and me out to dinner to celebrate my birthday, even though it was two weeks late. We had Mexican food and Coca-Cola and ice cream for dessert.

Dad gave me a pair of Rollerblades, and Lester gave me a disposable camera. I took a picture of him eating a tamale. He took a picture of me holding up my Rollerblades. There was a present from Aunt Sally, too. It was a box with bubble bath and dusting powder in it.

"What do I do with dusting powder?" I asked Dad. "Sprinkle it around my room?"

"You're supposed to put it on your feet when they stink," said Lester.

I won't ever believe another thing Lester tells me.

While we were eating our ice cream, though, I was thinking about Sara's family—the way the kids take care of themselves. If they could do that, so could we. I decided that sometime soon Lester and I would have to think of a really *good* way to get rid of Mrs. Nolinstock. Without even hurting her feelings, maybe.

20

Dropping the Baby

The last week of school is "last times" week. The last time the art teacher comes to our school. The last time we have music. The last time we get to play kickball at recess.

We don't learn very much. We learn who has to go to summer camp and who gets to stay home. We learn whose grandma is coming to visit and who has to share her bed with a cousin. We learn who gets to go to Kings Dominion or Disney World.

But the day before the very last day of school, during our very last science lesson, Mr. Dooley was talking about oceans and what we should look for if anyone was going to the beach during summer vacation. And right in the middle of our science lesson a woman came to the door of our room. She was holding a baby against her shoulder.

Mr. Dooley had been sitting on the edge of his desk telling us about sand crabs. He stood up with a big smile on his face.

"Well, class, I thought you might like to meet the little fellow we've known since he was a tiny embryo." He held out his arms for the baby and introduced his wife to the class.

I looked at the baby. I looked at Mrs. Dooley and wondered how a tiny little woman like her could have a big baby inside her. Elijah David was as big as a volleyball. Even bigger. I guess your skin really stretches when a baby is growing inside you.

Mr. Dooley sat down at his desk with Elijah on his lap. The baby was making little sucking sounds with his lips, and his blue eyes were looking about as we gathered around him. Every time Mr. Dooley moved his knee, Elijah David jumped and waved his tiny fists. Sara reached out one finger and put it in Elijah's hand. His fingers curled around it.

I wished *I* had done that! I didn't know that if you put your finger in a baby's hand, he would hold on. Sara moved her own finger up and down. The baby's hand went up and down, like he was directing a band. We laughed. I guess if you have as many brothers and sisters as Sara has, you learn a lot about babies.

"So here you have a human animal—and humans are mammals, you know; they drink their mother's milk," said Mr. Dooley. "This one grew inside his mother for nine months, and here he is. He has ten fingers . . ." Mr. Dooley smiled and pulled off the baby's booties. ". . . and ten toes . . ." He showed us Elijah's feet. ". . . two little ears . . . two eyes. . . . Isn't it remarkable that we have two of so many things in case something goes wrong with one of them? What else do we have two of, class?"

"Two legs," said Ollie.

"Two feet," said Donald.

"Lungs," said Jody.

"Kidneys," said Rosalind.

"But we only have one heart and one brain," I said.

"That's right, Alice. Those are two important things we have only one of, so we have to take special care of our hearts and our brains," said Mr. Dooley. He looked around. "Would anyone like to hold Elijah?"

I stared. This wonderful baby who had taken nine months to grow, and Mr. Dooley was going to let one of us *hold* him? Before I could blink, all the girls and even some of the boys were waving their hands. I raised mine too late. Mr. Dooley chose Megan. He let her sit in his desk chair and tucked Elijah in the crook of her arm.

While Megan held the baby, Mr. Dooley showed us Elijah's soft spot on the top of his head, and he told us how we had to be extra careful not to let a baby's head flop around. I wished that *I* were the one sitting there holding the baby. *Why* hadn't I been the first one with my hand in the air?

When the bell rang to go home, I felt as though I was going to cry. I think I wanted to hold Elijah David more than anyone else in the room wanted to hold him. Mrs. Dooley had taken him now, and all the kids were lining up to go home. I heard Mrs. Dooley tell her husband that she would wait for him in our library.

I decided I was not going home. If Mrs. Dooley was going to wait for Mr. Dooley, I would wait too. When the other kids went out the door, I slipped in the rest room and hid. I stayed until the hall was quiet. Then I went down to the library. Mrs. Dooley was sitting in a chair near the back. Oh no! She was holding Elijah to her chest, with a blanket covering his face, and I knew he was drinking from her breast.

I was such a blunderbuss! I didn't even guess that he might be nursing. I was ready to turn around and leave when Mrs. Dooley looked up and smiled at me. "Hi," she said.

"Hi," I answered.

"I'll bet you wanted to hold Elijah too, didn't you?"

She had blue eyes, just like her baby, but she had a lot more hair.

I nodded and walked over.

She buttoned her blouse and uncovered the baby's face. He had milk on his chin, and he looked very sleepy.

"Well, it's snack time for Elijah, but he needs to be burped," she said. "Do you want to sit next to me and I'll show you how to do it?"

I just grinned and sat down. I hoped my hands were clean.

Mrs. Dooley put Elijah against her, his face peeking out over her shoulder. She kept one hand behind his head and the other on his bottom. Then she gently jiggled him up and down.

When she put him in my arms, I tried to hold him just like that. I braced his bottom against my arm and put my other hand behind his head. I jiggled him gently up and down, just the way she had.

Elijah David was warm against me. He squirmed and made little grunting noises. My smile kept getting wider. Mrs. Dooley smiled too. So did the librarian, who was watching from her desk. I jiggled and patted the baby some more. And suddenly an enormous belch came from Elijah David. I didn't know a baby could make such a loud noise.

Baarrpt! went the baby.

Mrs. Dooley and the librarian and I all laughed.

Baarrpt! went Elijah again, not so loud this time.

"What a great burper you are!" Mrs. Dooley said. "I think that's about the best burp Elijah ever made."

I smiled all the way home that day. I even smiled at Mrs. Nolinstock. I wished the whole class had seen me holding Elijah David and heard his enormous burp.

"I got to hold a baby at school today and make him burp," I told Mrs. Nolinstock.

"Oh," she said. "That's one thing I didn't get that I always wanted: a baby."

I didn't know what to say. The woman in brown with the rubber band around her hair in back had never told me anything so personal before. I wondered if it was a secret.

I sat down on the couch in the living room and thought about it. Maybe that's why she liked to cook, I decided. Maybe she liked to go in other people's houses and feed them because she couldn't feed a little baby of her own.

"Guess what I am?" I said that night at dinner as we were eating the turkey and noodles that Mrs. Nolinstock had made.

"A girl?" said Lester. "The Creature from the Black Lagoon?"

"A terrific burper," I said.

Dad frowned a little. "I hope that's not something you were practicing at school."

I told him about Mr. Dooley's baby and how I got to make him burp.

"Oh," said Dad. "That's different."

When Oatmeal jumped up in my lap, I tried to show them how I had held Elijah to my shoulder, but cats don't belch. They scratch.

"I remember when you used to do that," said Lester.

"Scratch?" I asked.

"Belch," said Lester. "You used to belch so loud, I thought it was the door buzzer."

"Lester!" I scolded.

"You did! You used to belch so loud, I thought it was a jackhammer."

"You did not!"

"You used to belch so loud, the neighbors could hear you clear down the block," said Lester.

"I don't believe you now and I never will, ever again," I told him.

On the last day of school we helped Mr. Dooley clean up the classroom. We straightened the construction paper in the supply cupboard, put all the Magic Markers in the right boxes, and counted our playground stuff—the bats and balls and jump ropes—in the closet. It was my job to look for the two volleyballs with our room number on them. I found one under some burlap sacks in the closet, but I had to check the other classrooms to find the other one.

When I brought it back and took it into the supply closet, I thought how the volleyball was almost as big as Mr. Dooley's baby. Probably *exactly* the size of Elijah David when he was growing inside his mother.

I looked at the volleyball. I looked at my stomach. I pushed the volleyball down the front of my jumper till it got as far as my stomach. Was this what it was like to have a baby growing inside you? I wondered. I couldn't bend over. I couldn't even see my feet.

Suddenly Ollie came in the closet holding a couple of bats.

"Hey!" he yelled. "Look at Alice!"

Before I could push the volleyball on through, Jody and Dawn appeared in the doorway. Dawn shrieked with laughter.

"Look, everybody!" she cried. "Alice is pregnant."

I bopped the volleyball hard with my fist, and it finally slid on down my jumper and bounced on the floor, but not until more kids had gathered.

"Alice just had a baby!" Rosalind giggled.

"Yeah, she dropped it on the floor!" laughed Sara.

I could feel my cheeks starting to burn. Everyone was laughing and pointing at the volleyball, which rolled into a corner just as Mr. Dooley looked in.

"She had it down her dress!" Donald told Mr. Dooley, pointing.

"Let's put the stuff away now and clean out our desks," Mr. Dooley said. "And be sure to check the lost-and-found box for anything you might have lost this year."

I went back to my desk to throw out all my spelling papers. *Why do I do such silly things?* I wondered. On the very last day of school why couldn't I have made up a poem about Elijah and written it on the blackboard? Why couldn't I have drawn a picture of Mr. Dooley and his baby so we could all sign our names and wish him a happy summer?

Instead, the last thing anyone would remember about me was that I had stuffed a volleyball down my jumper and pretended I was having a baby.

21

The Cooking Lesson

The first morning of summer vacation Lester didn't even come up from the basement. I didn't blame him. I sort of wanted to spend the rest of my life in bed too with the covers up over my head. I hoped that everyone who had seen what I did with the volleyball would have either such a wonderful or such an awful summer that they would forget all about what I had done in the closet.

But I ate my cereal and drank my juice, and finally Mrs. Nolinstock asked me to go downstairs and see if my brother "intended" to eat any breakfast.

I went halfway down the steps and sat on the one that squeaked. I could see the lump that was Lester under the sheet. I moved one way on the step. *Creeaak,* it went. I moved the other way. *Craaack!*

Finally the lump said, "What d'ya want?"

"Mrs. Nolinstock wants to know if you intend to eat breakfast," I told him.

"Tell her I intend to stay in bed all day. This is vacation," Lester muttered.

"I thought you had a job at the miniature golf place," I said.

"I do. Seven to ten in the evenings."

"That means you have all day to do whatever you want," I said.

Lester rolled over. "Yeah? If I come upstairs, I'll run into *her*. And if I leave to get away from her, where am I supposed to go if I don't have a car?"

Now I began to get scared. What if Lester just packed his clothes and ran away? What if he saved up his money from the miniature golf job and bought a bus ticket to Louisiana or someplace?

I went down the rest of the steps and sat on the edge of his bed. "Lester," I said, "if we could do everything Mrs. Nolinstock does, Dad wouldn't have to hire her anymore. Right?"

"Yeah?" said Lester. "And how are we going to do that?"

"Well, she always takes her shoes off and lies down for a while after she finishes cooking. I could sneak out in the kitchen and copy some of her recipes, and we could cook them ourselves," I told him.

"Fine," said Lester, closing his eyes again. "You do that."

"And we could clean the house ourselves. I'll do the floors if you'll do the high places."

"Deal," said Lester. "You do the floors and the rugs and the bathtub and toilet, and I'll do the book-shelves."

That took care of cooking and cleaning, but Dad still had Lester and me to worry about, and I guess he worried plenty.

During the summer Mrs. Nolinstock was to spend all day at our house on Mondays, Wednesdays, Fridays, and Saturdays. We had Tuesdays and Thursdays to ourselves. Dad said that he would trust us to get along together then, that he wasn't going to ask Mrs. Sheavers to watch me during vacation. So I invited Rosalind to come over one Thursday and help me make spaghetti sauce. I had copied down Mrs. Nolinstock's recipe and was pretty certain we had everything we'd need, but I wasn't sure about some of her handwriting.

"Have you ever made spaghetti sauce?" I asked Rosalind.

"Nope," she said. "But it's probably got lots of ketchup in it."

I looked at the recipe. I didn't see any ketchup. I read

off the ingredients: "'One-half pound ground beef; one can tomato sauce; T. paste to thicken; onions . . .' I understand everything except 'T. paste to thicken,'" I said.

"A capital *T* stands for *tablespoon*," said Rosalind. "A lowercase *t* stands for *teaspoon*."

"Are you sure?" I asked.

"Positive," said Rosalind. "It looks like you're supposed to stir in a tablespoon of paste."

"Like school paste?"

"I guess so. It will make it thick, all right," said Rosalind.

"But can you *eat* it?" I asked.

"I used to eat paste in kindergarten and I'm still here," said Rosalind.

So we got out the ground beef and browned it in a big pot and added the tomato sauce and the spices, and when it began to bubble, I measured out a tablespoon of thick white paste from the jar I'd brought home from school. I'm not supposed to cook unless Lester is home, and Lester was home, all right. He just wasn't awake.

Actually, the spaghetti sauce looked pretty good until we put the paste in it. I thought it would dissolve and make the sauce thicker. Instead, little white lumps settled down over the top. Some of them began to foam.

"I think I'll be going home," said Rosalind.

"No, you won't!" I told her. "I invited you to stay for dinner. You can start making the salad."

By the time Lester came up from the basement and Dad came home from work, we had the sauce ready, and Dad boiled the spaghetti. There was a salad by every plate. I sprinkled Parmesan cheese on the sauce to hide the lumps.

"Smells good," said Dad.

"Mmm! Spaghetti!" said Lester. "I've only got twenty minutes to eat. Have to be at work by seven," he said. "Care if I go ahead?"

"Please do," said Rosalind, and put her hands in her lap. "You first."

We passed the bowl of spaghetti and then the sauce. I noticed that Rosalind kept digging through her serving, pushing little lumps of paste to one side.

A few minutes later, though, Dad stopped eating. He was pressing one finger against the lump on his plate—a big lump—about the size of a pea.

"What *is* this?" he asked. "Looks like something didn't dissolve."

"It's the thickening," I said, without raising my eyes.

"Cornstarch?" asked Dad. "Flour?"

Now Lester was smushing a lump on *his* plate. "Tastes like paste!" he said.

"It is. That's what Mrs. Nolinstock's recipe said," I told them. "A tablespoon of paste."

Dad looked at Rosalind, then at me. "Could I see that recipe?" he asked.

I got up and found it on the counter. Dad took his glasses out of his pocket and put them on.

"Al, this means tomato paste," he said. "The *T* stands for *tomato*. You can buy tomato paste in cans, just like tomato sauce, only it's thicker."

"Arrrgggghhh!" Lester cried, clutching his chest. "She poisoned me!"

I shot daggers across the table at Lester. How could Dad ever trust us to get along without Mrs. Nolinstock if he acted like that?

"I'm *really* going home now," said Rosalind. "Thanks for dinner, Alice." She got up and went home. Lester went out and drove away.

I looked at Dad. "I really am a blunderbuss," I said.

"Oh, I don't think so," he said. "At least you tried."

Tried to get rid of Mrs. Nolinstock, but of course I didn't tell him that.

Lester seemed to have a better plan for getting rid of her. Every Monday, Wednesday, and Friday afternoon that Mrs. Nolinstock was at our house, he invited the Naked Nomads to practice in our basement.

Our neighborhood was going to have a block party on the Fourth of July, and Lester's band had been invited to play. So Lester had an excuse to practice.

The first time they came, Mrs. Nolinstock looked relieved that they were all going down in the basement. But as soon as they plugged in their amplifiers and their electric guitars, as soon as the drums began to play, I could tell by the way she squinted her eyes and rubbed the skin over her temples that she had second thoughts about running the McKinley household.

The day of the party Rosalind came over because her brother is one of the Naked Nomads. And because Rosalind came, I invited Sara, too.

"Well, we ate paste and we're still alive," Rosalind told me. "What are we going to cook next?"

"*You* didn't eat any, Rosalind!" I said. "You just got me in trouble, that's all."

But it's hard to stay mad at Rosalind, so we went up and down the street, sampling the food that neighbors put out on card tables and watching the older kids dance. The Naked Nomads had set up their equipment in our yard next to the sidewalk, and every time they finished a song, people clapped.

Mrs. Nolinstock had baked a big cake with chocolate frosting, and everyone said what a marvelous cake it was. Mrs. Sheavers had made a big fruit salad, and she put it on the table right beside the cake. She didn't just set it down either. She sort of snuggled it up to the cake, like the McKinleys and the Sheaverses had made these desserts together, and somehow that made me nervous.

When Donald wasn't looking, I moved the fruit salad way over to the other side of the table and put a long row of plastic forks and spoons in between.

It was a good block party, though. After the Naked Nomads had played about three numbers, they took off their shirts, and the older girls who live on our block clapped when they saw that the boys had painted American flags on their chests.

When I walked by, one of the girls said, "Hey, aren't you Lester's sister?"

"Yes," I said.

The girls giggled. "So does he have anything painted on any other part of his body?" one of them asked.

I grinned. "Yeah," I said. "He's got the American eagle on his butt."

"Alice!" said Sara, poking me.

But Rosalind said, "Two eagles, one on each side."

The girls shrieked with laughter and moved toward the band. Rosalind and Sara and I laughed too and got out of there quick before someone told Lester. He wasn't the only one who could tell fibs!

I could see that he was having a *really* good time as the girls crowded around him. Lester had told Dad and me that Lisa Shane said she might come with one of her girlfriends. When I saw a red-haired girl I didn't

know smiling at him—a red-haired girl with a friend—
I decided I would go over and talk to her a little bit
when I had a chance so she would know I wasn't crazy
all the time.

When Rosalind and Sara went down the street to
get some potato salad and I saw the red-haired girl by
the lemonade stand, I walked over. "Hi. I'm Lester's
sister," I said. The girl and her friend stopped drinking and looked down at me. I decided I wouldn't
say anything about the box I'd sent her unless she
asked.

"You're Alice?" the red-haired girl said.

I smiled. "Yes. It's a nice block party, isn't it?"

She smiled too. "Yeah, it is. Lester said that his
friends were invited to hear him play, so Kim and I
dropped by."

I really wanted to help my brother. I wanted Lisa to
really, really like him even though he doesn't have a car.
Even though he has a sister who sticks her nose in his
business. "Well, he's awfully glad you're here, because
you're special," I said.

The girls looked at me and then at each other, laughing a little.

"Really?" the red-haired girl said.

"Yeah," I said. "He's sort of shy and—"

"*Lester? Shy?*" the girls both said together.

I began to wonder if I had said the right thing. "I

mean, he's okay now, but that's why Mom made him wait a year to start kindergarten."

"Wow!" exclaimed the friend named Kim. "It's hard to imagine."

I decided I'd better stop right there, so I just said, "But, anyway, it's nice to meet you."

"Nice to meet you, too," Kim said. "I'm glad Mickey told me about the party."

I froze. *Mickey?* The red-haired girl was *Mickey?* I had told Mickey Larson that *she* was special? "Good-bye," I said, and disappeared as fast as I could into the crowd.

The Naked Nomads were playing a fast number now, and as I passed our yard again, looking for Rosalind and Sara, I saw still another girl I didn't know, this one with brown hair, dancing with two other girls in front of Lester. The brown-haired girl was smiling at Lester as he played the drums, and he was smiling back. Maybe *that* was Lisa!

"Look at the crowd around Les," I heard the brown-haired girl say.

I will not throw up, I told myself, but I felt like it. I had just told Mickey Larson—the telephone pest—that she was special! And I could see her and her friend Kim standing next to the Naked Nomads, like worshippers in a church.

When I found Rosalind and Sara at last and told

them what I'd done, I asked if they thought I should go up to Lisa and tell her that *she* was special.

"Maybe you've done enough for one day," said Sara.

We sat down on the curb at the end of the block and watched balloons go up in the air. Someone was filling them with helium, but little kids kept letting them go by mistake. We went over and helped tie the balloons on to kids' wrists so they couldn't float off.

When I got up my nerve to go back toward our house again, there was a whole bunch of girls now crowded around the Naked Nomads, who were taking a break.

Lester was teaching the girl with the brown hair to hold a guitar and strum a few notes, and the other girls looked as though they were waiting their turn. The girl named Kim was joking with Rosalind's brother Billy, and Mickey was trying on Lester's shirt.

Maybe I hadn't ruined anything after all. Maybe the block party would be a nice thing that Lester could remember all his life. When the music started up again, Rosalind and Sara and I danced on the lawn. We held hands and whirled around and around, each of us leaning back as far as we could, till Rosalind suddenly let go of our hands and we all fell backward on the grass.

The sky was going around and around too, and we laughed. And then, after we caught our breath, we just stayed there in the grass, listening to the music and looking up at the clouds.

I crawled over and lay between Rosalind and Sara.

"Next year we'll all be fifth graders," I said.

"Yeah, but it won't be as much fun as fourth," said Sara.

"Fun?" I said. "Fourth grade was *fun*?"

"Sure," said Sara. "Remember the time the author burped into the microphone?"

"Remember the way Mr. Dooley's stomach growled?" said Rosalind.

We talked about Megan's sleep-over and my Christmas tree decorating party and Mr. Dooley's baby.

"Maybe it *was* a good year," I said. Not perfect, but okay.

22

Playing Tarzan

"I can't understand it," I heard Lester telling Dad the next morning. "The girls were swarming around us like flies! They sure must have liked the music."

Dad grinned.

"One of them said she really went for shy guys! Do I look like a shy guy to you?"

"You certainly don't. You looked like you were having a whale of a time yesterday," said Dad.

"And another girl wanted to know if I had a tattoo somewhere I wasn't telling. Man! That sure never happened back in Chicago!"

I walked into the kitchen in my pajamas just then and didn't say a word. I got down my cereal and poured the milk and kept my eyes on the bowl.

"How about you, Al? Did you have a good time at the party?" Dad asked.

"It was okay," I told him.

"I saw you whirling around with Rosalind and Sara," said Lester.

"Yeah. I spent almost the whole afternoon with them," I said.

"One of the girls said she met you," Lester added, reaching for the butter.

"Yeah?" I mumbled.

"She said you came over and talked for a while."

"There were so many people, I can't remember them all," I said.

When I went back to my room, I collapsed on the bed in relief. For once I had been a real blunderbuss and it had turned out perfectly A-okay!

Lester and I started to be friends again after that. Maybe it was because he realized I hadn't ruined things between him and Lisa Shane, or maybe it was because we both felt the same way about Mrs. Nolinstock.

One Saturday night in August, after Lester got home from his job at miniature golf, we sat up watching an old Tarzan movie.

Lester thought it was funny. He laughed all the way

through it. I thought it was the most exciting, the most romantic movie I had ever seen, and I didn't laugh at all.

In the part I liked best, Tarzan and Jane had just escaped a tribe of savages who were trying to kill them because they thought Tarzan had set fire to their village. Actually, lightning started the fire, but the savages didn't know that. So Tarzan and Jane leaped on this home-made raft, which was right there at the water's edge.

They were floating down the river, and Tarzan leaned over and kissed Jane. What they didn't know, though, was that there was a waterfall ahead, and the raft was traveling right toward it.

I screamed, "Look *out!*" but Lester just laughed, and the next thing I knew, Tarzan had grabbed Jane around the waist with one arm, and with the other hand, he grabbed a vine that just happened to be dangling from a tree and swung them both to safety.

I drew in my breath. In that moment I knew I just had to find out what it felt like to be kissed with my life in danger. I thought about it when I went to bed that night, and I was still thinking about it the next morning.

Maybe I was thinking about love and kisses because Aunt Sally had called again to say that Carol and her sailor were back from the honeymoon and that maybe it wouldn't be such a bad marriage after all. But as much as I wanted to be kissed with my life in danger, I certainly wasn't going to ask Lester to kiss me. So that afternoon when Donald came over, I said, "You want to be in the movies?"

"Yes," said Donald.

I found this big piece of cardboard that had come with our Sears washing machine, and I told Donald that this would be our raft. Then I explained about Tarzan and Jane and the lightning and the savages. I told him about the kissing, too, and we hung a jump rope over the lowest branch of the box elder tree so he could swing us to safety.

We figured out where the savages' village would be and planned our route through the jungle. We ran and screamed and climbed out of quicksand and leaped over alligators. At last we jumped onto the cardboard raft to escape down the river.

I was lying on my back, just like Jane.

Donald was resting on one elbow, just like Tarzan.

"Now?" asked Donald.

I nodded, but the very second he leaned over me, I got the giggles and rolled off.

"You fell into the river!" Donald said.

"Let's try it again," I told him.

So we went back to the savages' village, and there was this terrible thunderstorm, and just after lightning struck the huts, the savages all came out with their spears and they were yelling and we were running. And then we were on the raft again, and this time I closed my eyes, but I could tell that Donald was getting close to me because I could smell his bubble gum. I started to laugh again, and then, once more, I was in the water.

Donald was getting disgusted. "Stay on the raft!" he said. "How can I kiss you if you keep falling off into the water?"

I pressed my hands against my cheeks to squeeze the giggles off my face. "All right," I said seriously. "This time I will really truly do it."

So we went through the whole thing again, but by then the excitement was beginning to wear off. When the savages chased us, we didn't sound so scared anymore, and when we landed on the raft, I pressed my elbows down hard to make myself stay there.

As Donald bent over me again, though, I saw him going cross-eyed as he reached my nose, and just as the first giggle escaped from my mouth, I heard the side window open and Dad say, "Donald!" Donald rolled one way and I rolled another, and then a minute later Dad came around the side of the house.

"I don't think you should be doing that with Alice," he said. "You'd better go home, and the next time you come over, think of something else to do."

"Okay," said Donald.

I should have apologized to Donald. I should have told Dad it was all my idea. But I didn't. Dad put the cardboard out by the curb for the next day's trash pickup, and I decided I would stay in the house the whole rest of the summer because I could never face Donald Sheavers again.

"What's the matter with you?" Lester asked me later when I heard Donald calling to me from the porch and I went down in the basement to hide.

"I never want to see Donald Sheavers again," I told him.

"Well, you could always walk around with a bag over your head," he said.

"I wanted him to kiss me like Tarzan kissed Jane, and every time he tried it, I got the giggles," I said. "Do you ever get over embarrassing things that happen to you, Lester? Did you ever get over being embarrassed about kindergarten?"

"Kindergarten? What happened to me in kinder-garten?"

"Dad said that Mom waited till you were six to send you."

"Why should that embarrass me?"

I shrugged. "I don't know. I just thought maybe . . . because you're older . . ."

"Hey," said Lester, and he was smiling to himself now, "girls like to hang around with older guys, you know. Best decision Mom ever made."

Imagine that! I thought. Now that I'd told those girls he was older, that he had been held back because he was shy, he was more popular than ever. Sometimes I manage to do exactly the right thing!

Still, I avoided Donald Sheavers whenever I could. It was just too embarrassing. If he came out of his house, I went inside mine. Lester and I, though, were really busy. On the days that Mrs. Nolinstock didn't come, we tried some of her recipes. So far we had made chili with cheese and crackers, a Jell-O salad with raisins and carrots, a tuna noodle casserole, and deviled eggs. I was also making my bed each morning.

I scrubbed the kitchen floor once when Oatmeal's food got squashed into the linoleum, and Lester scrubbed the ring around the tub. We weren't sure whether or not Dad noticed. But one night when we had made spareribs for dinner, plus corn on the cob and an applesauce cake, Dad came home and said, "Mmm. Smells good!"

"Lester and I made the whole dinner ourselves," I said.

"Really?" said Dad. "I thought maybe this was something Mrs. Nolinstock left for us."

"It's her recipes, but we did the cooking," I explained.

"So? What's the occasion?" asked Dad.

"No occasion," Lester told him. "Al and I just thought we could do a little more around here in the culinary department."

"The what?" I asked.

"Cooking," said Lester.

"Well, I'm glad to hear it," said Dad, and immediately picked up a sparerib and began to eat.

Halfway through the meal Lester cleared his throat. "You know, Dad," he said, "my senior year is coming up, and Alice is ten. I really think you can let Mrs. Nolinstock go. Think of the money you'd be saving."

"Oh?" said Dad.

"Some of the other kids in my class take care of themselves after school, and they don't even have big brothers!" I said quickly.

"Who, exactly?" asked Dad.

"Well . . . uh . . . I'm not sure, but I know they do!" I fibbed.

"Les, what about the times you'd have things to do after school? You're going to be involved in a lot more activities, and I'm not about to send Alice to Mrs. Sheavers again. Donald's got no talent whatsoever for the trumpet, and the poor kid shouldn't have to take lessons just because his mom lets Alice come there. If I let Mrs. Nolinstock go, that means Alice is on her own five afternoons a week and all day on Saturday, with no one to keep an eye on her but you."

"Well, I'd rather be stuck with Alice sometimes than face Mrs. Nolinstock three times a week plus

Saturdays," said Lester. "She's the sphinx that never smiles, the parole officer who never jokes, the prison warden who never blinks."

She wasn't *that* bad, I thought, but I didn't dare say it.

Dad shook his head. "I don't know . . . I just don't know."

I began to feel worse and worse. All this trouble over me. *I* was the one who got trapped in the snow cave, who stuck a vitamin pill up her nose, who got caught waiting for Donald to kiss me. The only good thing that was happening was that the harder Lester and I worked to get rid of Mrs. Nolinstock, the closer we came to being friends again.

"Dad, I don't need anyone here!" I said. "I'm going into fifth grade and I have my own key and I've been cleaning the toilet and making my bed and I know how to cook and dial 911 and I won't let any stranger come inside when you're not here, not ever!"

"I'm impressed that you both are doing better with the meals, I really am," said Dad. "And I've noticed we have a cleaner tub and toilet. But it's not the cooking or the house I'm really worried about." He looked at me. "It's you . . . and Donald. And Lester . . . and . . ."

"Dad, Donald and I were playing Tarzan and it was all my idea and I wanted to know what it was like to be kissed with my life in danger and after the savages were after us we were supposed to jump on this raft except that—"

"I'm already confused enough, Al, don't repeat that," Dad said. He leaned back in his chair and looked first at me, then at Lester. "I'll tell you what: We'll try it for the month of September—just the two of you on your own. But if you have a friend over, I want to know about it in advance."

"Okay," said Lester, and stole a quick look at me.

"Sure!" I said.

"Al, I want you to come straight home from school each day and call me the minute you walk inside. Don't stop at anyone's house, and as soon as you get in, lock the door. You're not to turn on any stove or oven. Is that a promise?"

"Promise!" I said, nodding my head.

"And, Lester, anytime you need to be somewhere else after school, I want you to call Alice, see that she's okay, and let her know about what time you'll be home. Deal?"

"Deal," said Lester. We'd promise almost anything to get rid of Mrs. Nolinstock.

"As I said," Dad went on, "we'll try it for a month without Mrs. Nolinstock, and if things go reasonably well, we'll talk about making it permanent."

I ate like an adult for the rest of the meal. I wiped my mouth on my napkin, cleared the table, served the dessert, and rinsed off our dishes in the sink. But as soon as Dad left the kitchen, Lester and I grinned and gave each other a high five.

"Nice going, Alicia Katerina Makinoli," he said.

"You too, Dmitri Rachmaninoff Macaroni," I told him.

I wondered just how Dad would tell Mrs. Nolinstock the news. I'd never been around anyone being fired before. Would he wait until she had left some crumbs on the counter and then say, *Too bad, Mrs. Nolinstock, but I'm letting you go?* Would he wait until she got the beans too salty and say, *Mrs. Nolinstock, you're fired?*

I began to feel a little sorry for her. Maybe I would miss her. Was it possible? I *know* I would miss her cooking—her roast beef and browned potatoes. Lester and I had *never* tried to cook that! But though we waited and listened, we never heard Dad tell Mrs. Nolinstock he was letting her go. I decided that with the money I had saved for Lisa Shane, I would buy a pot holder for Mrs. Nolinstock, sort of a going-away present. She could use it when she found another family to feed.

I was almost too embarrassed to stay inside because I knew what was coming and she didn't. But I was even more embarrassed to go outside because I didn't want to run into Donald. I was tired of staying in the house all the time, though. I wished he'd get amnesia and forget everything we'd ever done together. That happens to people sometimes, I think, if they get hit on the head or something.

On the other hand, maybe he had forgotten already. Maybe Donald didn't remember anything over a week old.

On Wednesday, Mrs. Nolinstock asked me to take out the garbage. I picked up the sack and went out to the trash cans at the side of the house. There was Mrs. Sheavers coming down *her* back steps with her garbage at the same time.

"Hello, Alice!" she called. "I'll bet Mrs. Nolinstock is making you all her best dishes before she goes, isn't she?"

I paused with the lid of the garbage can in one hand. How did Mrs. Sheavers know we were firing Mrs. Nolinstock? How could she know that even before Mrs. Nolinstock knew it herself?

"How did you know?" I asked.

"Know what, dear?"

"That she was . . . leaving?" I said.

Mrs. Sheavers looked at me curiously. "Why, she and her husband are moving to Michigan in September. Your dad knew that before he hired her."

What? All this time Lester and I thought she was

going to be here for the rest of our lives, and Dad knew she was only here till September? All this time we had been cooking and cleaning and behaving ourselves just to show him we could do it, and all this time he *knew*?

Then I had another thought. An awful thought. If Lester and I didn't do a good job by ourselves, maybe Dad would hire someone *worse*! A real prison guard who couldn't cook!

At that moment Donald Sheavers came out on the steps. I wanted to run back in the house before he saw me. Jump in the garbage can, if I had to. But it was too late.

He threw back his head, thumped his chest, and gave a Tarzan yell.

This would go on forever, I thought. I would always do stupid things and people would never forget. And then I remembered that I was now ten years old and I was going to take care of myself after school. Not even Donald did that. Maybe I *had* stuffed a volleyball down my jumper and a pill up my nose, but I had also burped a baby and was friends again with Lester.

I looked at Donald Sheavers standing on his steps. I thumped *my* chest, threw back my head, and gave the loudest Tarzan yell ever. Then I went back in the house to tell Mrs. Nolinstock I liked her pies.